An Ambitious Man

Ella Wheeler Wilcox

Contents

AN AMBITIOUS MAN

BY

Ella Wheeler Wilcox

CHAPTER I

Preston Cheney turned as he ran down the steps of a handsome house on "The Boulevard," waving a second adieu to a young woman framed between the lace curtains of the window. Then he hurried down the street and out of view. The young woman watched him with a gleam of satisfaction in her pale blue eyes. A fine-looking young fellow, whose Roman nose and strong jaw belied the softly curved mouth with its sensitive darts at the corners; it was strange that something warmer than satisfaction did not shine upon the face of the woman whom he had just asked to be his wife.

But Mabel Lawrence was one of those women who are never swayed by any passion stronger than worldly ambition, never burned by any fires other than those of jealousy or anger. Her meagre nature was truly depicted in her meagre face. Nature is ofttimes a great lair and a cruel jester, giving to the cold and vapid woman the face and form of a sensuous siren, and concealing a heart of volcanic fires, or the soul of a Phryne, under the exterior of a spinster. But the old dame had been wholly frank in forming Miss Lawrence. The thin, flat chest and narrow shoulders, the angular elbows and prominent shoulder- blades, the sallow skin and sharp features, the deeply set, pale blue eyes, and the lustreless, ashen hair, were all truthful exponents of the unfurnished rooms in her vacant heart and soul places.

Miss Lawrence turned from the window, and trailed her long silken train across the rich carpet, seating herself before the open fireplace. It was an appropriate time and situation for a maiden's tender dreams; only a few hours had passed since the handsomest and most brilliant young man in that thriving eastern town had asked her to be his wife, and placed the kiss of betrothal upon her virgin lips. Yet it was with a sense of triumph and relief, rather than with tenderness and rapture, that the young woman meditated upon the situation--triumph over other women who had shown a decided interest in Mr Cheney, since his arrival in the place more than eighteen months ago, and relief that the dreaded role of spinster was not to be her part in life's drama.

Miss Lawrence was twenty-six--one year older than her fiance; and she had never received a proposal of marriage or listened to a word of love in her life before. Let me transpose that phrase--she had never before received a proposal of marriage, and had never in her life listened to a word of love; for Preston had not spoken of love. She knew that he did not love her. She knew that he had sought her hand wholly from ambitious motives. She was the daughter of the Hon. Sylvester Lawrence, lawyer, judge, state senator, and proposed candidate for lieutenant-governor in the coming campaign. She was the only heir to his large fortune.

Preston Cheney was a penniless young man from the West. A self-made youth, with an unusual brain and an overwhelming ambition, he had risen from chore boy on a western farm to printer's apprentice in a small town, thence to reporter, city editor, foreign correspondent, and after two or three years of travel gained in this manner he had come to Beryngford and bought out a struggling morning paper, which was making a mad effort to keep alive, changed its political tendencies, infused it with western activity and filled it with cosmopolitan news, and now, after eighteen months, the young man found himself coming abreast of his two long established rivals in the editorial field. This success was but an incentive to his overwhelming ambition for place, power and riches. He had seen just enough of life and of the world to estimate these things at double their value; and he was, beside, looking at life through the magnifying glass of youth. The Creator intended us to gaze on worldly possessions and selfish ambitions through the small end of the lorgnette, but youth invariably inverts the glass.

To the young editor, the brief years behind him seemed like a long hard pull up a steep and rocky cliff. From the point to which he had attained, the summit of his desires looked very far away, much farther than the level from which he had arisen. To rise to that summit single-handed and alone would require unremitting effort through the very best years of his manhood. His brain, his strength, his ability, his ambitions, what were they all in the strife after place and power, compared to the money of some commonplace adversary? Preston Cheney, the native-born American directly descended from a Revolutionary soldier, would be handicapped in the race with some Michael Murphy whose father had made a fortune in the saloon business, or who had himself acquired a competency as a police officer.

America was not the same country which gave men like Benjamin Franklin, Abraham Lincoln and Horace Greeley a chance to rise from the lower ranks to the highest places before they reached middle life. It was no longer a land where merit strove with merit, and the prize fell to the most earnest and the most gifted. The tremendous influx of foreign population since the war of the Rebellion and the right of franchise given unreservedly to the illiterate and the vicious rendered the ambitious American youth now a toy in the hands of aliens, and position a thing to be bought at the price set by un- American masses.

Thoughts like these had more and more with each year filled the mind of Preston Cheney, until, like the falling of stones and earth into a river bed, they changed the naturally direct current of his impulses into another channel. Why not further his life purpose by an ambitious marriage? The first time the thought entered his mind he had cast it out as something unclean and unworthy of his manhood. Marriage was a holy estate, he said to himself, a sacrament to be entered into with reverence, and sanctified by love. He must love the woman who was to be the companion of his life, the mother of his children.

Then he looked about among his early friends who had married, as nearly all the young men of the middle classes in America do marry, for love, or what they believed to be love. There was Tom Somers--a splendid lad, full of life, hope and ambition when he married Carrie Towne, the prettiest girl in Vandalia. Well, what was he now, after seven years? A broken-spirited man, with a sickly, complaining wife and a brood of ill-clad children. Harry Walters, the most infatuated lover he had ever seen, was divorced after five years of discordant marriage.

Charlie St Clair was flagrantly unfaithful to the girl he had pursued three years with his ardent wooings before she yielded to his suit. Certainly none of these love marriages were examples for him to follow. And in the midst of these reveries and reflections, Preston Cheney came to Beryngford, and met Sylvester Lawrence and his daughter Mabel. He met also Berene Dumont. Had he not met the latter woman he would not have succumbed--so soon at least--to the temptation held out by the former to advance his ambitious aims.

He would have hesitated, considered, and reconsidered, and without doubt his better nature and his good taste would have prevailed. But when fate threw Berene Dumont in his way, and circumstances brought about his close associations with her for many months, there seemed but one way of escape from the Scylla of his desires, and that was to the Charybdis of a marriage with Miss Lawrence.

Miss Lawrence was not aware of the part Berene Dumont had played in her engagement, but she knew perfectly the part her father's influence and wealth had played; but she was quite content with affairs as they were, and it mattered little to her what had brought them about. To be married, rather than to be loved, had been her ambition since she left school; being incapable of loving, she was incapable of appreciating the passion in any of its phases. It had always seemed to her that a great deal of nonsense was written and talked about love. She thought demonstrative people very vulgar, and believed kissing a means of conveying germs of disease.

But to be a married woman, with an establishment of her own, and a husband to exhibit to her friends, was necessary to the maintenance of her pride.

When Miss Lawrence's mother, a nervous invalid, was informed of her daughter's engagement, she burst into tears, as over a lamb offered on the altar of sacrifice; and Judge Lawrence pressed a kiss on the lobe of Mabel's left ear which she offered him, and told her she had won a prize in the market. But as he sat alone over his cigar that night, he sighed heavily, and said to himself, "Poor fellow, I wish Mabel were not so much like her mother."

CHAPTER II

Baroness Brown" was a distinctive figure in Beryngford. She came to the place from foreign parts some three years before the arrival of Preston Cheney, and brought servants, carriages and horses, and established herself in a very handsome house which she rented for a term of years. Her arrival in this quiet village town was of course the sensation of the hour, or rather of the year. She was known as Baroness Le Fevre--an American widow of a French baron. Large, voluptuous, blonde, and handsome according to the popular idea of beauty, distinctly amiable, affable and very charitable, she became at once the fashion.

Invitations to her house were eagerly sought after, and her entertainments were described in column articles by the press.

This state of things continued only six months, however. Then it began to be whispered about that the Baroness was in arrears for her rent. Several of her servants had gone away in a high state of temper at the titled mistress who had failed to pay them a cent of wages since they came to the country with her; and one day the neighbours saw her fine carriage horses led away by the sheriff.

A week later society was electrified by the announcement of the marriage of Baroness Le Fevre to Mr Brown, a wealthy widower who owned the best shoe store in Beryngford.

Mr Brown owned ten children also, but the youngest was a boy of sixteen, absent in college. The other nine were married and settled in comfortable homes.

Mr Brown died at the expiration of a year. This one year had taught him more of womankind than he had learned in all his sixty and nine years before; and, feeling that it is never too late to profit by learning, Mr Brown discreetly made his will, leaving all his property save the widow's "thirds" equally divided among his ten children.

The Baroness made a futile effort to break the will, on the ground that he was not of sound mind when it was drawn up; but the effort cost her several hundred of her few thousand dollars and the increased enmity of the ten Brown children, and availed her nothing. An important part of the widow's third was the Brown mansion, a large, commodious house built many years before, when the village was but a country town. Everybody supposed the Baroness, as she was still called, half in derision and half from the American love of mouthing a title, would offer this house for sale, and depart for fresh fields and pastures new. But the Baroness never did what she was expected to do.

Instead of offering her house for sale, she offered "Rooms to Let," and turned the family mansion into a fashionable lodging-house.

Its central location, and its adjacence to several restaurants and boarding houses, rendered it a convenient place for business people to lodge, and the handsome widow found no trouble in filling her rooms with desirable and well-paying patrons. In a spirit of fun, people began to speak of the old Brown mansion as "The Palace," and in a short time the lodging-house was known by that name, just as its mistress was known as "Baroness Brown."

The Palace yielded the Baroness something like two hundred dollars a month, and cost her only the wages and keeping of three servants; or rather the wages of two and the keeping of three; for to Berene Dumont, her maid and personal attendant, she paid no wages.

The Baroness did not rise till noon, and she always breakfasted in bed. Sometimes she remained in her room till mid-afternoon. Berene served her breakfast and lunch, and looked after the servants to see that the lodgers' rooms were all in order. These were the services for which she was given a home. But in truth the young woman did much more than this; she acted also as seamstress and milliner for her mistress, and attended to the marketing and ran errands for her. If ever a girl paid full price for her keeping, it was Berene, and yet the Baroness spoke frequently of "giving the poor thing a home."

It had all come about in this way. Pierre Dumont kept a second-hand book store in Beryngford. He was French, and the national characteristic of frugality had assumed the shape of avarice in his nature. He was, too, a petty tyrant and a cruel husband and father when under the influence of absinthe, a state in which he was usually to be found.

Berene was an only child, and her mother, whom she worshipped, said, when dying, "Take care of your poor father, Berene. Do everything you can to make him happy. Never desert him."

Berene was fourteen at that time. She had never been at school, but she had been taught to read and write both French and English, for her mother was an American girl who had been disinherited by her grandparents, with whom she lived, for eloping with her French teacher--Pierre Dumont. Rheumatism and absinthe turned the French professor into a shopkeeper before Berene was born. The grandparents had died without forgiving their granddaughter, and, much as the unhappy woman regretted her foolish marriage, she remained a patient and devoted wife to the end of her life, and imposed the same patience and devotion when dying on her daughter.

At sixteen, Berene was asked to sacrifice herself on the altar of marriage to a man three times her age; one Jacques Letellier, who offered generously to take the young girl as payment for a debt owed by his convivial comrade, M. Dumont. Berene wept and begged piteously to be spared this horrible sacrifice of her young life, whereupon Pierre Dumont seized his razor and threatened suicide as the other alternative from the dishonour of debt, and Berene in terror yielded her word and herself the next day to the debasing mockery of marriage with a depraved old gambler and roue.

Six months later Jacques Letellier died in a fit of apoplexy and Berene was freed from her chains; but freed only to keep on in a life of martyrdom as servant and slave to the caprices of her father, until his death. When he was finally well buried under six feet of earth, Berene found herself twenty years of age, alone in the world with just one thousand dollars in money, the price brought by her father's effects.

Without education or accomplishments, she was the possessor of youth, health, charm, and a voice of wonderful beauty and power; a voice which it was her dream to cultivate, and use as a means of support. But how could she ever cultivate it? The thousand dollars in her possession was, she knew, but a drop in the ocean of expense a musical education would entail. And she must keep that money until she found some way by which to support herself.

Baroness Brown had attended the sale of old Dumont's effects. She had often noticed the young girl in the shop, and in the street, and had been struck with the peculiar elegance and refinement of her appearance. Her simple lawn or print gowns were made and worn in a manner befitting a princess. Her nails were carefully kept, despite all the household drudgery which devolved upon her.

The Baroness was a shrewd woman and a clever reasoner. She needed a thrifty, prudent person in her house to look after things, and to attend to her personal needs. Since she had opened the Palace as a lodging-house, this need had stared her in the face. Servants did very well in their places, but the person she required was of another and superior order, and only to be obtained by accident or by advertising and the paying of a large salary. Now the Baroness had been in the habit of thinking that her beauty and amiability were quite equivalent to any favours she received from humanity at large. Ever since she was a plump girl in short dresses, she had learned that smiles and compliments from her lips would purchase her friends of both sexes, who would do disagreeable duties for her. She had never made it a custom to pay out money for any service she could obtain otherwise. So now as she looked on this young woman who, though a widow, seemed still a mere child, it occurred to her that Fate had with its usual kindness thrown in her path the very person she needed.

She offered Berene "a home" at the Palace in return for a few small services. The lonely girl, whose strangely solitary life with her old father had excluded her from all social relations outside, grasped at this offer from the handsome lady whom she had long admired from a distance, and went to make her home at the Palace.

CHAPTER III

Berene had been several months in her new home when Preston Cheney came to lodge at the Palace.

He met her on the stairway the first morning after his arrival, as he was descending to the street door.

Bringing up a tray covered with a snowy napkin, she stepped to one side and paused, to make room for him to pass.

Preston was not one of those young men who find pastime in flirtations with nursery maids or kitchen girls. The very thought of it offended his good taste. Once, in listening to the boastful tales of a modern Don Juan, who was relating his gallant adventures with a handsome waiter girl at a hotel, Preston had remarked, "I would as soon think of using my dinner napkin for a necktie, as finding romance with a servant girl."

Yet he appreciated a snowy, well-laundried napkin in its place, and he was most considerate and thoughtful in his treatment of servants.

He supposed Berene to be an upper servant of the house, and yet, as he glanced at her, a strange and unaccountable feeling of interest seized upon him. The creamy pallor of her skin, colourless save for the full red lips, the dark eyes full of unutterable longing, the aristocratic poise of the head, the softly rounded figure, elegant in its simple gown and apron, all impressed him as he had never before been impressed by any woman.

It was several days before he chanced to see her again, and then only for a moment as she passed through the hall; but he heard a trill of song from her lips, which added to his interest and curiosity. "That girl is no common servant," he said to himself, and he resolved to learn more about her.

It had been the custom of the Baroness to keep herself quite hidden from her lodgers. They seldom saw her, after the first business interview. Therefore it was a matter of surprise to the young editor when he came home from his office one night, just after twelve o'clock, and found the mistress of the mansion standing in the hall by the register, in charming evening attire.

She smiled upon him radiantly. "I have just come in from a benefit concert," she said, "and I am as hungry as a bear. Now I cannot endure eating alone at night. I knew it was near your hour to return, so I waited for you. Will you go down to the dining-room with me and have a Welsh rarebit? I am going to make one in my chafing dish."

The young man hid his surprise under a gallant smile, and offering the Baroness his arm descended to the basement dining-room with her. He had heard much about the complicated life of this woman, and he felt a certain amount of natural curiosity in regard to her. He had met her but once, and that was on the day when he had called to engage his room, a little more than two weeks past.

He had thought her an excellent type of the successful American adventuress on that occasion, and her quiet and dull life in this ordinary town puzzled him. He could not imagine a woman of that order existing a whole year without an adventure; as a rule he knew that those blonde women with large hips and busts, and small waists and feet, are as unable to live without excitement as a fish without water.

Yet, since the death of Mr Brown, more than a year past, the Baroness had lived the life of a recluse. It puzzled him, as a student of human nature.

But, in fact, the Baroness was a skilled general in planning her campaigns. She seldom plunged into action unprepared.

She knew from experience that she could not live in a large city and not use an enormous amount of money.

She was tired of taking great risks, and she knew that without the aid of money and a fine wardrobe she was not able to attract men as she had done ten years before.

As long as she remained in Beryngford she would be adding to her income every month, and saving the few thousands she possessed. She would be saving her beauty, too, by keeping early hours and living a temperate life; and if she carefully avoided any new scandal, her past adventures would be dim in the minds of people when, after a year or two more of retirement and retrenchment, she sallied forth to new fields, under a new name, if need be, and with a comfortably filled purse.

It was in this manner that the Baroness had reasoned; but from the hour she first saw Preston Cheney, her resolutions wavered. He impressed her most agreeably; and after learning about him from the daily papers, and hearing him spoken of as a valuable acquisition to Beryngford's intellectual society, the Baroness decided to come out of her retirement and enter the lists in advance of other women who would seek to attract this newcomer.

To the fading beauty in her late thirties, a man in the early twenties possesses a peculiar fascination; and to the Baroness, clothed in weeds for a husband who died on the eve of his seventieth birthday, the possibility of winning a young man like Preston Cheney overbalanced all other considerations in her mind. She had never been a vulgar coquette to whom all men were prey. She had always been more or less discriminating. A man must be either very attractive or very rich to win her regard. Mr Brown had been very rich, and Preston Cheney was very attractive.

"He is more than attractive, he is positively FASCINATING," she said to herself in the solitude of her room after the tete-a-tete over the Welsh rarebit that evening. "I don't know when I have felt such a pleasure in a man's presence. Not since--" But the Baroness did not allow herself to go back so far. "If there is any fruit I DETEST, it is DATES," she often said laughingly. "Some people delight in a good memory--I delight in a good forgettory of the past, with its telltale milestones of birthdays and anniversaries of marriages, deaths and divorces."

"Mr Cheney said I looked very young to have been twice married. Twice!" and she laughed aloud before her mirror, revealing the pink arch of her mouth, and two perfect sets of yellow-white teeth, with only one blemishing spot of gold visible. "I wonder if he meant it, though?" she mused. "And the fact that I DO wonder is the sure proof that I am really interested in this man. As a rule, I never believe a word men say, though I delight in their flattery all the same. It makes me feel comfortable even when I know they are lying. But I should really feel hurt if I thought Mr Cheney had not meant what he said. I don't believe he knows much about women, or about himself lower than his brain. He has never studied his heart. He is all ambition. If an ambitious and unsophisticated youth of twenty-five or twenty-eight does get infatuated with a woman of my age--he is a perfect toy in her hands. Ah, well, we shall see what we shall see." And the Baroness finished her massage in cold cream, and put her blonde head on the pillow and went sound asleep.

After that first tete-a-tete supper the fair widow managed to see Preston at least once or twice a week. She sent for him to ask his advice on business matters, she asked him to aid her in changing the position of the furniture in a room when the servants were all busy, and she invited him to her private parlour for lunch every Sunday afternoon. It was during one of these chats over cake and wine that the young man spoke of Berene. The Baroness had dropped some remarks about her servants, and Preston said, in a casual tone of voice which hid the real interest he felt in the subject, "By the way, one of your servants has quite an unusual voice. I have heard her singing about the halls a few times, and it seems to me she has real talent."

"Oh, that is Miss Dumont--Berene Dumont--she is not an absolute servant," the Baroness replied; "she is a most unfortunate young woman to whom my heart went out in pity, and I have given her a home. She is really a widow, though she refuses to use her dead husband's name."

"A widow?" repeated Preston with surprise and a queer sensation of annoyance at his heart; "why, from the glimpse I had of her I thought her a young girl."

"So she is, not over twenty-one at most, and woefully ignorant for that age," the Baroness said, and then she proceeded to outline Berene's history, laying a good deal of stress upon her own charitable act in giving the girl a home.

"She is so ignorant of life, despite the fact that she has been married, and she is so uneducated and helpless, I could not bear to see her cast into the path of designing people," the Baroness said. "She has a strong craving for an education, and I give her good books to read, and good advice to ponder over, and I hope in time to come she will marry some honest fellow and settle down to a quiet, happy home life. The man who brings us butter and eggs from the country is quite fascinated with her, but she does not deign him a glance." And then the Baroness talked of other things.

But the history he had heard remained in Preston Cheney's mind and he could not drive the thought of this girl away. No wonder her eyes were sad! Better blood ran in her veins than coursed under the pink flesh of the Baroness, he would wager; she was the unfortunate victim of a combination of circumstances, which had defrauded her of the advantages of youth.

He spoke with her in the hall one morning not long after that; and then it grew to be a daily occurrence that he talked with her a few moments, and before many weeks had passed the young man approached the Baroness with a request.

"I have become interested in your protegee Miss Dumont," he said. "You have done so much for her that you have stirred my better nature and made me anxious to emulate your example. In talking with her in the hall one day I learned her great desire for a better education, and her anxiety to earn money. Now it has occurred to me that I might aid her in both ways. We need two or three more girls in our office. We need one more in the type-setting department. As The Clarion is a morning paper, and you never need Miss Dumont's services after five o'clock, she could work a few hours in the office, earn a small salary, and gain something in the way of an education also, if she were ambitious enough to do so. Nearly all my early education was gained as a printer. She tells me she is faulty in the matter of spelling, and this would be excellent training for her. You have, dear madam, inspired the girl with a desire for more knowledge, and I hope you will let me carry on the good work you have begun."

Preston had approached the matter in a way that could not fail to bring success--by flattering the vanity and pride of the Baroness. So elated was she with the agreeable references to herself, that she never suspected the young man's deep personal interest in the girl. She believed in the beginning that he was showing Berene this kind attention solely to please the mistress.

Berene entered the office as type-setter, and made such astonishing progress that she was promoted to the position of proof-reader ere six months had passed. And hour by hour, day by day, week by week, the strange influence which she had exerted on her employer, from the first moment of their meeting, grew and strengthened, until he realised with a sudden terror that his whole being was becoming absorbed by an intense passion for the girl.

Meantime the Baroness was growing embarrassing in her attentions. The young man was not conceited, nor prone to regard himself as an object of worship to the fair sex. He had during the first few months believed the Baroness to be amusing herself with his society. He had not flattered himself that a woman of her age, who had seen so much of the world, and whose ambitions were so unmistakable, could regard him otherwise than as a diversion.

But of late the truth had forced itself upon him that the woman wished to entangle him in a serious affair. He could not afford to jeopardise his reputation at the very outset of his career by any such entanglement, or by the appearance of one. He cast about for some excuse to leave the Palace, yet this would separate him in a measure from his association with Berene, beside incurring the enmity of the Baroness, and possibly causing Berene to suffer from her anger as well.

He seemed to be caught like a fly in a net. And again the thought of his future and his ambitions confronted him, and he felt abashed in his own eyes, as he realised how far away these ambitions had seemed of late, since he had allowed his emotions to overrule his brain.

What was this ignorant daughter of a French professor, that she should stand between him and glory, riches and power? Desperate diseases needed desperate remedies. He had been an occasional caller at the Lawrence homestead ever since he came to Beryngford. Without being conceited on the subject, he realised that Mabel Lawrence would not reject him as a suitor.

The masculine party is very dull, or the feminine very deceptive, when a man makes a mistake in his impressions on this subject.

That afternoon the young editor left his office at five o'clock and asked Miss Lawrence to be his wife.

CHAPTER IV

Preston Cheney walked briskly down the street after he left his fiancee, his steps directed toward the Palace. It was seven o'clock, and he knew the Baroness would be at home.

He had determined upon heroic treatment for his own mental disease (as he regarded his peculiar sentiments toward Berene Dumont), and he had decided upon a similar course of treatment for the Baroness.

He would confide his engagement to her at once, and thus put an end to his embarrassing position in the Palace, as well as to establish his betrothal as a fact-- and to force himself to so regard it. It was strange reasoning for a young man in the very first hour of his new role of bridegroom elect, but this particular groom elect had deliberately placed himself in a peculiar position, and his reasoning was not, of course, that of an ardent and happy lover.

Already he was galled by his new fetters; already he was feeling a sense of repulsion toward the woman he had asked to be his wife: and because of these feelings he was more eager to nail himself hand and foot to the cross he had builded.

He was obliged to wait some time before the Baroness came into the reception-room; and when she came he observed that she had made an elaborate toilet in his honour. Her sumptuous shoulders billowed over the low-cut blue corsage like apple-dumplings over a china dish. Her waist was drawn in to an hourglass taper, while her ample hips spread out beneath like the heavy mason work which supports a slender column. Tiny feet encased in pretty slippers peeping from beneath her silken skirts looked oddly out of proportion with the rest of her generous personality, and reminded Preston of the grotesque cuts in the humorous weeklies, where well-known politicians were represented with large heads and small extremities. Artistic by nature, and with an eye to form, he had never admired the Baroness's type of beauty, which was the theme of admiration for nearly every other man in Beryngford. Her face, with its infantine colouring, its large, innocent azure eyes, and its short retrousse features, he conceded to be captivatingly pretty, however, and it seemed unusually so this evening. Perhaps because he had so recently looked upon the sharp, sallow face of his fiancee.

Preston frequently came to his room about this hour, after having dined and before going to the office for his final duties; but he seldom saw the Baroness on these occasions, unless through her own design.

"You were surprised to receive my message, no doubt, saying I wished to see you," he began. "But I have something I feel I ought to tell you, as it may make some changes in my habits, and will of course eventually take me away from these pleasant associations." He paused for a second, and the Baroness, who had seated herself on the divan at his side, leaned forward and looked inquiringly in his face.

"You are going away?" she asked, with a tremor in her voice. "Is it not very sudden?"

"No, I am not going away," he replied, "not from Beryngford--but I shall doubt-less leave your house ere many months. I am engaged to be married to Miss Mabel Lawrence. You are the first person to whom I have imparted the news, but you have been so kind, and I feel that you ought to know it in time to secure a desirable tenant for my room."

Again there was a pause. The rosy face of the Baroness had grown quite pale, and an unpleasant expression had settled about the corners of her small mouth. She waved a feather fan to and fro languidly. Then she gave a slight laugh and said:

"Well, I must confess that I am surprised. Miss Lawrence is the last woman in the world whom I would have imagined you to select as a wife. Yet I congratulate you on your good sense. You are very ambitious, and you can rise to great distinc-tion if you have the right influence to aid you. Judge Lawrence, with his wealth and position, is of all men the one who can advance your interests, and what more natu-ral than that he should advance the interests of his son-in-law? You are a very wise youth and I again congratulate you. No romantic folly will ever ruin your life."

There was irony and ridicule in her voice and face, and the young man felt his cheek tingle with anger and humiliation. The Baroness had read him like an open book--as everyone else doubtless would do. It was bitterly galling to his pride, but there was nothing to do, save to keep a bold front, and carry out his role with as much dignity as possible.

He rose, spoke a few formal words of thanks to the Baroness for her kindness to him, and bowed himself from her presence, carrying with him down the street the memory of her mocking eyes.

As he entered his private office, he was amazed to see Berene Dumont sitting in his chair fast asleep, her head framed by her folded arms, which rested on his desk. Against the dark maroon of her sleeve, her classic face was outlined like a marble statuette. Her long lashes swept her cheek, and in the attitude in which she sat, her graceful, perfectly-proportioned figure displayed each beautiful curve to the best advantage.

To a noble nature, the sight of even an enemy asleep, awakes softening emotions, while the sight of a loved being in the unconsciousness of slumber stirs the fountain of affection to its very depths.

As the young editor looked upon the girl before him, a passion of yearning love took possession of him. A wild desire to seize her in his arms and cover her pale face with kisses, made his heart throb to suffocation and brought cold beads to his brow; and just as these feelings gained an almost uncontrollable dominion over his reason, will and judgment, the girl awoke and started to her feet in confusion.

"Oh, Mr Cheney, pray forgive me!" she cried, looking more beautiful than ever with the flush which overspread her face. "I came in to ask about a word in your editorial which I could not decipher. I waited for you, as I felt sure you would be in shortly--and I was so TIRED I sat down for just a second to rest--and that is all I knew about it. You must forgive me, sir!--I did not mean to intrude."

Her confusion, her appealing eyes, her magnetic voice were all fuel to the fire raging in the young man's heart. Now that she was for ever lost to him through his own deliberate action, she seemed tenfold more dear and to be desired. Brain, soul, and body all seemed to crave her; he took a step forward, and drew in a quick breath as if to speak; and then a sudden sense of his own danger, and an overwhelming disgust for his weakness swept over him, and the intense passion the girl had aroused in his heart changed to unreasonable anger.

"Miss Dumont," he said coldly, "I think we will have to dispense with your services after to-night. Your duties are evidently too hard for you. You can leave the office at any time you wish. Good-night."

The girl shrank as if he had struck her, looked up at him with wide, wondering eyes, waited for a moment as if expecting to be recalled, then, as Mr Cheney wheeled his chair about and turned his back upon her, she suddenly sped away without a word.

She left the office a few moments later; but it was not until after eleven o'clock that she dragged herself up two flights of stairs toward her room on the attic floor at the Palace. She had been walking the streets like a mad creature all that intervening time, trying to still the agonising pain in her heart. Preston Cheney had long been her ideal of all that was noble, grand and good, she worshipped him as devout pagans worshipped their sacred idols; and, without knowing it, she gave him the absorbing passion which an intense woman gives to her lover.

It was only now that he had treated her with such rough brutality, and discharged her from his employ for so slight a cause, that the knowledge burst upon her tortured heart of all he was to her.

She paused at the foot of the third and last flight of stairs with a strange dizziness in her head and a sinking sensation at her heart.

A little less than half-an-hour afterwards Preston Cheney unlocked the street door and came in for the night. He had done double his usual amount of work and had finished his duties earlier than usual. To avoid thinking after he sent Berene away, he had turned to his desk and plunged into his labour with feverish intensity. He wrote a particularly savage editorial on the matter of over-immigration, and his leaders on political questions of the day were all tinctured with a bitterness and sarcasm quite new to his pen. At midnight that pen dropped from his nerveless hand, and he made his way toward the Palace in a most unenviable state of mind and body.

Yet he believed he had done the right thing both in engaging himself to Miss Lawrence and in discharging Berene. Her constant presence about the office was of all things the most undesirable in his new position.

"But I might have done it in a decent manner if I had not lost all control of myself," he said as he walked home. "It was brutal the way I spoke to her; poor child, she looked as if I had beat her with a bludgeon. Well, it is just as well perhaps that I gave her good reason to despise me."

Since Berene had gone into the young man's office as an employe her good taste and another reason had caused her to avoid him as much as possible in the house. He seldom saw more than a passing glimpse of her in the halls, and frequently whole days elapsed that he met her only in the office. The young man never suspected that this fact was due in great part to the suggestion of jealousy in the manner of the Baroness toward the young girl ever after he had shown so much interest in her welfare. Sensitive to the mental atmosphere about her, as a wind harp to the lightest breeze, Berene felt this unexpressed sentiment in the breast of her "benefactress" and strove to avoid anything which could aggravate it.

With a lagging step and a listless air, Preston made his way up the first of two flights of stairs which intervened between the street door and his room. The first floor was in darkness; but in the upper hall a dim light was always left burning until his return. As he reached the landing, he was startled to see a woman's form lying at the foot of the attic stairs, but a few feet from the door of his room. Stooping down, he uttered a sudden exclamation of pained surprise, for it was upon the pallid, unconscious face of Berene Dumont that his eyes fell. He lifted the lithe figure in his sinewy arms, and with light, rapid steps bore her up the stairs and in through the open door of her room.

"If she is dead, I am her murderer," he thought. But at that moment she opened her eyes and looked full into his, with a gaze which made his impetuous, uncontrolled heart forget that any one or anything existed on earth but this girl and his love for her.

CHAPTER V

One of the greatest factors in the preservation of the Baroness's beauty had been her ability to sleep under all conditions. The woman who can and does sleep eight or nine hours out of each twenty-four is well armed against the onslaught of time and trouble.

To say that such women do not possess heart enough or feeling enough to suffer is ofttimes most untrue.

Insomnia is a disease of the nerves or of the stomach, rather than the result of extreme emotion. Sometimes the people who sleep the most profoundly at night in times of sorrow, suffer the more intensely during their waking hours. Disguised as a friend, deceitful Slumber comes to them only to strengthen their powers of suffering, and to lend a new edge to pain.

The Baroness was not without feeling. Her temperament was far from phlegmatic. She had experienced great cyclones of grief and loss in her varied career, though many years had elapsed since she had known what the French call a "white night."

But the night following her interview with Preston Cheney she never closed her eyes in sleep. It was in vain that she tried all known recipes for producing slumber. She said the alphabet backward ten times; she counted one thousand; she conjured up visions of sheep jumping the time-honoured fence in battalions, yet the sleep god never once drew near.

"I am certainly a brilliant illustration of the saying that there is no fool like an old fool," she said to herself as the night wore on, and the strange sensation of pain and loss which Preston Cheney's unexpected announcement had caused her gnawed at her breast like a rat in a wainscot.

That she had been unusually interested in the young editor she knew from the first; that she had been mortally wounded by Cupid's shaft she only now discovered. She had passed through a divorce, two "affairs" and a legitimate widowhood, without feeling any of the keen emotions which now drove sleep from her eyes. A long time ago, longer than she cared to remember, she had experienced such emotions, but she had supposed such folly only possible in the high tide of early youth. It was absurd, nay more, it was ridiculous to lie awake at her time of life thinking about a penniless country youth whose mother she might almost have been. In this bitterly frank fashion the Baroness reasoned with herself as she lay quite still in her luxurious bed, and tried to sleep.

Yet despite her frankness, her philosophy and her reasoning, the rasping hurt at her heart remained--a hurt so cruel it seemed to her the end of all peace or pleasure in life.

It is harder to bear the suffocating heat of a late September day which the year sometimes brings, than all the burning June suns.

The Baroness heard the click of Preston's key in the street door, and she listened to his slow step as he ascended the stairs. She heard him pause, too, and waited for the sound of the opening of his room door, which was situated exactly above her own. But she listened in vain, her ears, brain and heart on the alert with surprise, curiosity, and at last suspicion. The Baroness was as full of curiosity as a cat.

It was not until just before dawn that she heard his step in the hall, and his door open and close.

An hour later a sharp ring came at the street door bell. A message for Mr Preston, the servant said, in answer to her mistress's question as she descended from the room above.

"Was Mr Preston awake when you rapped on his door?" asked the Baroness.

"Yes, madame, awake and dressed."

Mr Preston ran hurriedly through the halls and out to the street a moment later; and the Baroness, clothed in a dressing-gown and silken slippers, tiptoed lightly to his room. The bed had not been occupied the whole night. On the table lay a note which the young man had begun when interrupted by the message which he had thrown down beside it.

The Baroness glanced at the note, on which the ink was still moist, and read, "My dear Miss Lawrence, I want you to release me from the ties formed only yesterday--I am basely unworthy--" here the note ended. She now turned her attention to the message which had prevented the completion of the letter. It was signed by Judge Lawrence and ran as follows:-

"My Dear Boy,--My wife was taken mortally ill this morning just before day-break. She cannot live many hours, our physician says. Mabel is in a state of complete nervous prostration caused by the shock of this calamity. I wish you would come to us at once. I fear for my dear child's reason unless you prove able to calm and quiet her through this ordeal. Hasten then, my dear son; every moment before you arrive will seem an age of sorrow and anxiety to me. "S. LAWRENCE."

A strange smile curved the corners of the Baroness's lips as she finished reading this note and tiptoed down the stairs to her own room again.

Meantime the hour for her hot water arrived, and Berene did not appear. The Baroness drank a quart of hot water every morning as a tonic for her system, and another quart after breakfast to reduce her flesh. Her excellent digestive powers and the clear condition of her blood she attributed largely to this habit.

After a few moments she rang the bell vigorously. Maggie, the chambermaid, came in answer to the call.

"Please ask Miss Dumont" (Berene was always known to the other servants as Miss Dumont) "to hurry with the hot water," the Baroness said.

"Miss Dumont has not yet come downstairs, madame."

"Not come down? Then will you please call her, Maggie?"

The Baroness was always polite to her servants. She had observed that a graciousness of speech toward her servants often made up for a deficiency in wages. Maggie ascended to Miss Dumont's room, and returned with the information that Miss Dumont had a severe headache, and begged the indulgence of madame this morning.

Again that strange smile curved the corners of the Baroness's lips.

Maggie was requested to bring up hot water and coffee, and great was her surprise to find the Baroness moving about the room when she appeared with the tray.

Half-an-hour later Berene Dumont, standing by an open window with her hands clasped behind her head, heard a light tap on her door. In answer to a mechanical "Come," the Baroness appeared.

The rustle of her silken morning gown caused Berene to turn suddenly and face her; and as she met the eyes of her visitor the young woman's pallor gave place to a wave of deep crimson, which dyed her face and neck like the shadow of a red flag falling on a camellia blossom.

"Maggie tells me you are ill this morning," the Baroness remarked after a moment's silence. "I am surprised to find you up and dressed. I came to see if I could do anything for you."

"You are very kind," Berene answered, while in her heart she thought how cruel was the expression in the face of the woman before her, and how faded she appeared in the morning light. "But I think I shall be quite well in a little while, I only need to keep quiet for a few hours."

"I fear you passed a sleepless night," the Baroness remarked with a solicitous tone, but with the same cruel smile upon her lips. "I see you never opened your bed. Something must have been in the air to keep us all awake. I did not sleep an hour, and Mr Cheney never entered his room till near morning. Yet I can understand his wakefulness--he announced his engagement to Miss Mabel Lawrence to me last evening, and a young man is not expected to woo sleep easily after taking such an important step as that. Judge Lawrence sent for him a few hours ago to come and support Miss Mabel during the trial that the day is to bring them in the death of Mrs Lawrence. The physician has predicted the poor invalid's near end. Sorrow follows close on joy in this life."

There was a moment's silence; then Miss Dumont said: "I think I will try to get a little sleep now, madame. I thank you for your kind interest in me."

The Baroness descended to her room humming an air from an old opera, and settled to the task of removing as much as possible all evidences of fatigue and sleeplessness from her countenance.

It has been said very prettily of the spruce-tree, that it keeps the secret of its greenness well; so well that we hardly know when it sheds its leaves. There are women who resemble the spruce in their perennial youth, and the vigilance with which they guard the secret of it. The Baroness was one of these. Only her mirror shared this secret.

She was an adept at the art of preservation, and greatly as she disliked physical exertion, she toiled laboriously over her own person an hour at least every day, and never employed a maid to assist her. One's rival might buy one's maid, she reasoned, and it was well to have no confidant in these matters.

She slipped off her dressing-gown and corset and set herself to the task of pinching and mauling her throat, arms and shoulders, to remove superfluous flesh, and strengthen muscles and fibres to resist the flabby tendencies which time produces. Then she used the dumb- bells vigorously for fifteen minutes, and that was followed by five minutes of relaxation. Next she lay on the floor flat upon her face, her arms across her back, and lifted her head and chest twenty-five times. This exercise was to replace flesh with muscle across the abdomen. Then she rose to her feet, set her small heels together, turned her toes out squarely, and, keeping her body upright bent her knees out in a line with her hips, sinking and rising rapidly fifteen times. This produced pliancy of the body, and induced a healthy condition of the loins and adjacent organs.

To further fight against the deadly enemy of obesity, she lifted her arms above her head slowly until she touched her finger tips, at the same time rising upon her tiptoes, while she inhaled a long breath, and as slowly dropped to her heels, and lowered her arms while she exhaled her breath. While these exercises had been taking place, a tin cup of water had been coming to the boiling point over an alcohol lamp. This was now poured into a china bowl containing a small quantity of sweet milk, which was always brought on her breakfast tray.

The Baroness seated herself before her mirror, in a glare of cruel light which revealed every blemish in her complexion, every line about the mouth and eyes.

"You are really hideously passee, mon amie," she observed as she peered at herself searchingly; "but we will remedy all that."

Dipping a soft linen handkerchief in the bowl of steaming milk and water, she applied it to her face, holding it closely over the brow and eyes and about the mouth, until every pore was saturated and every weary drawn tissue fed and strengthened by the tonic. After this she dashed ice-cold water over her face. Still there were little folds at the corners of the eyelids, and an ugly line across the brow, and these were manipulated with painstaking care, and treated with mysterious oils and fragrant astringents and finally washed in cool toilet water and lightly brushed with powder, until at the end of an hour's labour, the face of the Baroness had resumed its roseleaf bloom and transparent smoothness for which she was so famous. And when by the closest inspection at the mirror, in the broadest light, she saw no flaw in skin, hair, or teeth, the Baroness proceeded to dress for a drive. Even the most jealous rival would have been obliged to concede that she looked like a woman of twenty- eight, that most fascinating of all ages, as she took her seat in the carriage.

In the early days of her life in Beryngford, when as the Baroness Le Fevre she had led society in the little town, Mrs Lawrence had been one of her most devoted friends; Judge Lawrence one of her most earnest, if silent admirers. As "Baroness Brown" and as the landlady of "The Palace" she had still maintained her position as friend of the family, and the Lawrences, secure in their wealth and power, had allowed her to do so, where some of the lower social lights had dropped her from their visiting lists.

The Baroness seemed to exercise a sort of hypnotic power over the fretful, nervous invalid who shared Judge Lawrence's name, and this influence was not wholly lost upon the Judge himself, who never looked upon the Baroness's abundant charms, glowing with health, without giving vent to a profound sigh like some hungry child standing before a confectioner's window.

The news of Mrs Lawrence's dangerous illness was voiced about the town by noon, and therefore the Baroness felt safe in calling at the door to make inquiries, and to offer any assistance which she might be able to render. Knowing her intimate relations with the mistress of the house, the servant admitted her to the parlour and announced her presence to Judge Lawrence, who left the bedside of the invalid to tell the caller in person that Mrs Lawrence had fallen into a peaceful slumber, and that slight hopes were entertained of her possible recovery. Scarcely had the words passed his lips, however, when the nurse in attendance hurriedly called him. "Mrs Lawrence is dead!" she cried. "She breathed only twice after you left the room."

The Baroness, shocked and startled, rose to go, feeling that her presence longer would be an intrusion.

"Do not go," cried the Judge in tones of distress. "Mabel is nearly distracted, and this news will excite her still further. We thought this morning that she was on the verge of serious mental disorder. I sent for her fiance, Mr Cheney, and he has calmed her somewhat. You always exerted a soothing and restful influence over my wife, and you may have the same power with Mabel. Stay with us, I beg of you, through the afternoon at least."

The Baroness sent her carriage home and remained in the Lawrence mansion until the following morning. The condition of Miss Lawrence was indeed serious. She passed from one attack of hysteria to another, and it required the constant attention of her fiance and her mother's friend to keep her from acts of violence.

It was after midnight when she at last fell asleep, and Preston Cheney in a state of complete exhaustion was shown to a room, while the Baroness remained at the bedside of Miss Lawrence.

When the Baroness and Mr Cheney returned to the Palace they were struck with consternation to learn that Miss Dumont had packed her trunk and departed from Beryngford on the three o'clock train the previous day.

A brief note thanking the Baroness for her kindness, and stating that she had imposed upon that kindness quite too long, was her only farewell. There was no allusion to her plans or her destination, and all inquiry and secret search failed to find one trace of her. She seemed to vanish like a phantom from the face of the earth.

No one had seen her leave the Palace, save the laundress, Mrs Connor; and little this humble personage dreamed that Fate was reserving for her an important role in the drama of a life as yet unborn.

CHAPTER VI

Whatever hope of escape from his self-imposed bondage Preston Cheney had entertained when he began the note to his fiancee which the Baroness had read, completely vanished during the weeks which followed the death of Mrs Lawrence.

Mabel's nervous condition was alarming, and her father seemed to rely wholly upon his future son-in-law for courage and moral support during the trying ordeal. Like most large men of strong physique, Judge Lawrence was as helpless as an infant in the presence of an ailing woman; and his experience as the husband of a wife whose nerves were the only notable thing about her, had given him an absolute terror of feminine invalids.

Mabel had never been very fond of her mother; she had not been a loving or a dutiful daughter. A petulant child and an irritable, fault-finding young woman, who had often been devoid of sympathy for her parents, she now exhibited such an excess of grief over the death of her mother that her reason seemed to be threatened.

It was, in fact, quite as much anger as grief which caused her nervous paroxysms. Mabel Lawrence had never since her infancy known what it was to be thwarted in a wish. Both parents had been slaves to her slightest caprice and she had ruled the household with a look or a word. Death had suddenly deprived her of a mother who was necessary to her comfort and to whose presence she was accustomed, and her heart was full of angry resentment at the fate which had dared to take away a member of her household. It had never entered her thoughts that death could devastate HER home.

Other people lost fathers and mothers, of course; but that Mabel Lawrence could be deprived of a parent seemed incredible. Anger is a strong ingredient in the excessive grief of every selfish nature.

Preston Cheney became more and more disheartened with the prospect of his future, as he studied the character and temperament of his fiancee during her first weeks of loss.

But the net which he had woven was closing closer and closer about him, and every day he became more hopelessly entangled in its meshes.

At the end of one month, the family physician decided that travel and change of air and scene was an imperative necessity for Miss Lawrence. Judge Lawrence was engaged in some important legal matters which rendered an extended journey impossible for him. To trust Mabel in the hands of hired nurses alone, was not advisable. It was her father who suggested an early marriage and a European trip for bride and groom, as the wisest expedient under the circumstances.

Like the prisoner in the iron room, who saw the walls slowly but surely closing in to crush out his life, Preston Cheney saw his wedding day approaching, and knew that his doom was sealed.

There were many desperate hours, when, had he possessed the slightest clue to the hiding-place of Berene Dumont, he would have flown to her, even knowing that he left disgrace and death behind him. He realised that he now owed a duty to the girl he loved, higher and more imperative by far than any he owed to his fiancee. But he had not the means to employ a detective to find Berene; and he was not sure that, if found, she might not spurn him. He had heard and read of cases where a woman's love had turned to bitter loathing and hatred for the man who had not protected her in a moment of weakness. He could think of no other cause which would lead Berene to disappear in such a mysterious manner at such a time, and so the days passed and he married Mabel Lawrence two months after the death of her mother, and the young couple set forth immediately on extended foreign travels. Fifteen months later they returned to Beryngford with their infant daughter Alice. Mrs Cheney was much improved in health, though still a great sufferer from nervous disorders, a misfortune which the child seemed to inherit. She would lie and scream for hours at a time, clenching her small fists and growing purple in the face, and all efforts of parents, nurses or physicians to soothe her, served only to further increase her frenzy. She screamed and beat the air with her thin arms and legs until nature exhausted itself, then she fell into a heavy slumber and awoke in good spirits.

These attacks came on frequently in the night, and as they rendered Mrs Cheney very "nervous," and caused a panic among the nurses, it devolved upon the unhappy father to endeavour to soothe the violent child. And while he walked the floor with her or leaned over her crib, using all his strong mental powers to control these unfortunate paroxysms, no vision came to him of another child lying cuddled in her mother's arms in a distant town, a child of wonderful beauty and angelic nature, born of love, and inheriting love's divine qualities.

A few months before the young couple returned to their native soil, they received a letter which caused Preston the greatest astonishment, and Mabel some hours of hysterical weeping. This letter was written by Judge Lawrence, and announced his marriage to Baroness Brown. Judge Lawrence had been a widower more than a year when the Baroness took the book of his heart, in which he supposed the hand of romance had long ago written "finis," and turning it to his astonished eyes revealed a whole volume of love's love.

It is in the second reading of their hearts that the majority of men find the most interesting literature.

Before the Baroness had been three months his wife, the long years of martyrdom he had endured as the husband of Mabel's mother seemed like a nightmare dream to Judge Lawrence; and all of life, hope and happiness was embodied in the woman who ruled his destiny with a hypnotic sway no one could dispute, yet a woman whose heart still throbbed with a stubborn and lawless passion for the man who called her husband father.

CHAPTER VII

More than two decades had passed since Preston Cheney followed the dictates of his ambition and married Mabel Lawrence.

Many of his early hopes and desires had been realised during these years. He had attained to high political positions; and honour and wealth were his to enjoy. Yet Senator Cheney, as he was now known, was far from a happy man. Disappointment was written in every lineament of his face, restlessness and discontent spoke in his every movement, and at times the spirit of despair seemed to look from the depths of his eyes.

To a man of any nobility of nature, there can be small satisfaction in honours which he knows are bought with money and bribes; and to the proud young American there was the additional sting of knowing that even the money by which his honours were purchased was not his own.

It was the second Mrs Lawrence (still designated as the "Baroness" by her stepdaughter and by old acquaintances) to whom Preston owed the constant reminder of his dependence upon the purse of his father-in- law. In those subtle, occult ways known only to a jealous and designing nature, the Baroness found it possible to make Preston's life a torture, without revealing her weapons of warfare to her husband; indeed, without allowing him to even smell the powder, while she still kept up a constant small fire upon the helpless enemy.

Owing to the fact that Mabel had come as completely under the hypnotic influence of the Baroness as the first Mrs Lawrence had been during her lifetime, Preston was subjected to a great deal more of her persecutions than would otherwise have been possible. Mabel was never happier than when enjoying the companionship of her new mother; a condition of things which pleased the Judge as much as it made his son-in-law miserable.

With a malicious adroitness possible only to such a woman as the second Mrs Lawrence, she endeared herself to Mrs Cheney, by a thousand flattering and caressing ways, and by a constant exhibition of sympathy, which to a weak and selfish nature is as pleasing as it is distasteful to the proud and strong. And by this inexhaustible flow of sympathetic feeling, she caused the wife to drift farther and farther away from her husband's influence, and to accuse him of all manner of shortcomings and faults which had not suggested themselves to her own mind.

Mabel had not given or demanded a devoted love when she married Preston Cheney. She was quite satisfied to bear his name, and do the honours of his house, and to be let alone as much as possible. It was the name, not the estate, of wifehood she desired; and motherhood she had accepted with reluctance and distaste.

Never was a more undesired or unwelcome child born than her daughter Alice, and the helpless infant shared with its father the resentful anger which dominated her unwilling mother the wretched months before its advent into earth life.

To be let alone and allowed to follow her own whims and desires, and never to be crossed in any wish, was all Mrs Cheney asked of her husband.

This role was one he had very willingly permitted her to pursue, since with every passing week and month he found less and less to win or bind him to his wife. Wretched as this condition of life was, it might at least have settled into a monotonous calm, undisturbed by strife, but for the molesting "sympathy" of the Baroness.

"Poor thing, here you are alone again," she would say on entering the house where Mabel lounged or lolled, quite content with her situation until the tone and words of her stepmother aroused a resentful consciousness of being neglected. Again the Baroness would say:

"I do think you are such a brave little darling to carry so smiling a face about with all you have to endure." Or, "Very few wives would bear what you bear and hide every vestige of unhappiness from the world. You are a wonderful and admirable character in my eyes." Or, "It seems so strange that your husband does not adore you--but men are blind to the best qualities in women like you. I never hear Mr Cheney praising other women without a sad and almost resentful feeling in my heart, realising how superior you are to all of his favourites." It was the insidious effect of poisoned flattery like this, which made the Baroness a ruling power in the

Cheney household, and at the same time turned an already cold and unloving wife into a jealous and nagging tyrant who rendered the young statesman's home the most dreaded place on earth to him, and caused him to live away from it as much as possible.

His only child, Alice, a frail, hysterical girl, devoid of beauty or grace, gave him but little comfort or satisfaction. Indeed she was but an added disappointment and pain in his life. Indulged in every selfish thought by her mother and the Baroness, peevish and petulant, always ailing, complaining and discontented, and still a victim to the nervous disorders inherited from her mother, it was small wonder that Senator Cheney took no more delight in the role of father than he had found in the role of husband.

Alice was given every advantage which money could purchase. But her delicate health had rendered systematic study of any kind impossible, and her twentieth birthday found her with no education, with no use of her reasoning or will powers, but with a complete and beautiful wardrobe in which to masquerade and air her poor little attempts at music, art, or conversation.

Judge Lawrence died when Alice was fifteen years of age, leaving both his widow and his daughter handsomely provided for.

The Baroness not only possessed the Beryngford homestead, but a house in Washington as well; and both of these were occupied by tenants, for Mabel insisted upon having her stepmother dwell under her own roof. Senator Cheney had purchased a house in New York to gratify his wife and daughter, and it was here the family resided, when not in Washington or at the seaside resorts. Both women wished to forget, and to make others forget, that they had ever lived in Beryngford. They never visited the place and never referred to it. They desired to be considered "New Yorkers" and always spoke of themselves as such.

The Baroness was now hopelessly passee. Yet it was the revealing of the inner woman, rather than the withering of the exterior, which betrayed her years. The woman who understands the art of bodily preservation can, with constant toil and care, retain an appearance of youth and charm into middle life; but she who would pass that dreaded meridian, and still remain a goodly sight for the eyes of men, must possess, in addition to all the secrets of the toilet, those divine elixirs, unselfishness and love for humanity. Faith in divine powers, too, and resignation to earthly ills, must do their part to lend the fading eye lustre and to give a softening glow to the paling cheek. Before middle life, it is the outer woman who is seen; after middle life, skilled as she may be by art and however endowed my nature, yet the inner woman becomes visible to the least discerning eye, and the thoughts and feelings which have dominated her during all the past, are shown upon her face and form like printed words upon the open leaves of a book. That is why so many young beauties become ugly old ladies, and why plain faces sometimes are beautiful in age.

The Baroness had been unremitting in the care of her person, and she had by this toil saved her figure from becoming gross, retaining the upright carriage and the tapering waist of youth, though she was upon the verge of her sixtieth birthday. Her complexion, too, owing to her careful diet, her hours of repose, and her knowledge of skin foods and lotions, remained smooth, fair and unfurrowed. But the long-guarded expression in her blue eyes of childlike innocence had given place to the hard look of a selfish and unhappy nature, and the lines about the small mouth accented the expression of the eyes.

It was, despite its preservation of Nature's gifts, and despite its forced smiles, the face of a selfish, cruel pessimist, disappointed in her past and with no uplifting faith to brighten the future.

The Baroness had been the wife of Judge Lawrence a number of years, before she relinquished her hopes of one day making Preston Cheney respond to the passion which burned unquenched in her breast. It had been with the idea of augmenting the interests of the man whom she believed to be her future lover, that she aided and urged on her husband in his efforts to procure place and honour for his son-in- law.

It was this idea which caused her to widen the breach between wife and husband by every subtle means in her power; and it was when this idea began to lose colour and substance and drop away among the wreckage of past hopes, that the Baroness ceased to compliment and began to taunt Preston Cheney with his dependence upon his father-in- law, and to otherwise goad and torment the unhappy man. And Preston Cheney grew into the habit of staying anywhere longer than at home.

During the last ten years the Baroness had seemed to abandon all thoughts of gallant adventure. When the woman who has found life and pleasures only in co-quetry and conquest is forced to relinquish these delights, she becomes either very devout or very malicious.

The Baroness was devoid of religious feelings, and she became, therefore, the most bitter and caustic of cynical critics at heart, though she guarded her expression of these sentiments from policy.

Yet to Mabel she expressed herself freely, knowing that her listener enjoyed no conversation so much as that of gossip and criticism. A beautiful or attractive woman was the target for her most cruel shafts of sarcasm, and indeed no woman was safe from her secret malice save Mabel and Alice, over whom she found it a greater pleasure to exercise her hypnotic control. For Alice, indeed, the Baroness entertained a peculiar affection. The fact that she was the child of the man to whom she had given the strongest passion of her life, and the girl's lack of personal beauty, and her unfortunate physical condition, awoke a medley of love, pity and protection in the heart of this strange woman.

CHAPTER VIII

The Baroness had always been a churchgoing woman, yet she had never united with any church, or subscribed to any creed.

Religious observance was only an implement of social warfare with her. Wherever her lot was cast, she made it her business to discover which church the fashionable people of the town frequented, and to become a familiar and liberal-handed personage in that edifice.

Judge Lawrence and his family were High Church Episcopalians, and the second Mrs Lawrence slipped gracefully into the pew vacated by the first, and became a much more important feature in the congregation, owing to her good health and extreme desire for popularity. Mabel and Alice were devout believers in the orthodox dogmas which have taken the place of the simple teachings of Christ in so many of our churches to-day. They believed that people who did not go to church would stand a very poor chance of heaven; and that a strict observance of a Sunday religion would ensure them a passport into God's favour. When they returned from divine service and mangled the character and attire of their neighbours over the Sunday dinner- table, no idea entered their heads or hearts that they had sinned against the Holy Ghost. The pastor of their church knew them to be selfish, worldly-minded women; yet he administered the holy sacrament to them without compunction of conscience, and never by question or remark implied a doubt of their true sincerity in things religious. They believed in the creed of his church, and they paid liberally for the support of that church. What more could he ask?

This had been true of the pastor in Beryngford, and it proved equally true of their spiritual adviser in Washington and in New York.

Just across the aisle from the Lawrences sat a rich financier, in his sumptuously cushioned pew. During six days of each week he was engaged in crushing life and hope out of the hearts of the poor, under his juggernaut wheels of monopoly. His name was known far and near, as that of a powerful and cruel speculator, who did not hesitate to pauperise his nearest friends if they placed themselves in his reach. That he was a thief and a robber, no one ever denied; yet so colossal were his thefts, so bold and successful his robberies, the public gazed upon him with a sort of stupefied awe, and allowed him to proceed, while miserable tramps, who stole overcoats or robbed money drawers, were incarcerated for a term of years, and then sternly refused assistance afterward by good people, who place no confidence in jail birds.

But each Sunday this successful robber occupied his high-priced church pew, devoutly listening to the divine word.

He never failed to partake of the holy communion, nor was his right to do so ever questioned.

The rector of the church knew his record perfectly; knew that his gains were ill-gotten blood money, ground from the suffering poor by the power of monopoly, and from confiding fools by smart lures and scheming tricks. But this young clergyman, having recently been called to preside over the fashionable church, had no idea of being so impolite as to refuse to administer the bread and wine to one of its most liberal supporters!

There were constant demands upon the treasury of the church; it required a vast outlay of money to maintain the splendour and elegance of the temple which held its head so high above many others; and there were large charities to be sustained, not to mention its rector's princely salary. The millionaire pewholder was a liberal giver. It rarely occurs to the fashionable dispensers of spiritual knowledge to ask whether the devil's money should be used to gild the Lord's temple; nor to question if it be a wise religion which allows a man to rob his neighbours on weekdays, to give to the cause of charity on Sundays.

And yet if every clergyman and priest in the land were to make and maintain these standards for their followers, there might be an astonishing decrease in the needs of the poor and unfortunate.

Were every church member obliged to open his month's ledgers to a competent jury of inspectors, before he was allowed to take the holy sacrament and avow himself a humble follower of Christ, what a revolution might ensue! How church spires would crumble for lack of support, and poorhouses lessen in number for lack of inmates!

But the leniency of clergymen toward the shortcomings of their wealthy parishioners is often a touching lesson in charity to the thoughtful observer who stands outside the fold.

For how could they obtain money to convert the heathen, unless this sweet cloak of charity were cast over the sins of the liberal rich? Christ is crucified by the fashionable clergymen to-day more cruelly than he was by the Jews of old.

Senator Cheney was not a church member, and he seldom attended service. This was a matter of great solicitude to his wife and daughter. The Baroness felt it to be a mistake on the part of Senator Cheney, and even Judge Lawrence, who adored his son-in-law, regretted the young man's indifference to things spiritual. But with all Preston Cheney's worldly ambitions and weaknesses, there was a vein of sincerity in his nature which forbade his feigning a faith he did not feel; and the daily lives of the three feminine members of his family were so in disaccord with his views of religion that he felt no incentive to follow in their footsteps. Judge Lawrence he knew to be an honest, loyal-hearted, God and humanity loving man. "A true Christian by nature and education," he said of his father-in- law, "but I am not born with his tendency to religious observance, and I see less and less in the churches to lead me into the fold. It seems to me that these religious institutions are getting to be vast monopolistic corporations like the railroads and oil trusts, and the like. I see very little of the spirit of Christ in orthodox people to-day."

Meanwhile Senator Cheney's purse was always open to any demand the church made; he believed in churches as benevolent if not soul-saving institutions, and cheerfully aided their charitable work.

The rector of St Blank's, the fashionable edifice where the ladies of the Cheney household obtained spiritual manna in New York, died when Alice was sixteen years old. He was a good old man, and a sincere Episcopalian, and whatever originality of thought or expression he may have lacked, his strict observance of the High Church code of ethics maintained the tone of his church and rendered him an object of reverence to his congregation. His successor was Reverend Arthur Emerson Stuart, a young man barely thirty years of age, heir to a comfortable fortune, gifted with strong intellectual powers and dowered with physical attractions.

It was not a case of natural selection which caused Arthur Stuart to adopt the church as a profession. It was the result of his middle name. Mrs Stuart had been an Emerson--in some remote way her family claimed relationship with Ralph Waldo. Her father and grandfather and several uncles had been clergymen. She married a broker, who left her a rich widow with one child, a son. From the hour this son was born his mother designed him for the clergy, and brought him up with the idea firmly while gently fixed in his mind.

Whatever seed a mother plants in a young child's mind, carefully watches over, prunes and waters, and exposes to sun and shade, is quite certain to grow, if the soil is not wholly stony ground.

Arthur Stuart adored his mother, and stifling some commercial instincts inherited from the parental side, he turned his attention to the ministry and entered upon his chosen work when only twenty- five years of age. Eloquent, dramatic in speech, handsome, and magnetic in person, independent in fortune, and of excellent lineage on the mother's side, it was not surprising that he was called to take charge of the spiritual welfare of fashionable St Blank's Church on the death of the old pastor; or that, having taken the charge, he became immensely popular, especially with the ladies of his congregation. And from the first Sabbath day when they looked up from their expensive pew into the handsome face of their new rector, there was but one man in the world for Mabel Cheney and her daughter Alice, and that was the Reverend Arthur Emerson Stuart.

It has been said by a great and wise teacher, that we may worship the god in the human being, but never the human being as God. This distinction is rarely drawn by women, I fear, when their spiritual teacher is a young and handsome man. The ladies of the Rev. Arthur Stuart's congregation went home to dream, not of the Creator and Maker of all things, nor of the divine Man, but of the handsome face, stalwart form and magnetic voice of the young rector. They feasted their eyes upon his agreeable person, rather than their souls upon his words of salvation. Disappointed wives, lonely spinsters and romantic girls believed they were coming nearer to spiritual truths in their increased desire to attend service, while in fact they were merely drawn nearer to a very attractive male personality.

There was not the holy flame in the young clergyman's own heart to ignite other souls; but his strong magnetism was perceptible to all, and they did not realise the difference. And meantime the church grew and prospered amazingly.

It was observed by the congregation of St Blank's Church, shortly after the advent of the new rector, that a new organist also occupied the organ loft; and inquiry elicited the fact that the old man who had officiated in that capacity during many years, had been retired on a pension, while a young lady who needed the position and the salary had been chosen to fill the vacancy.

That the change was for the better could not be questioned. Never before had such music pealed forth under the tall spires of St Blank's. The new organist seemed inspired; and many people in the fashionable congregation, hearing that this wonderful musician was a young woman, lingered near the church door after service to catch a glimpse of her as she descended from the loft.

A goodly sight she was, indeed, for human eyes to gaze upon. Young, of medium height and perfectly symmetry of shape, her blonde hair and satin skin and eyes of velvet darkness were but her lesser charms. That which riveted the gaze of every beholder, and drew all eyes to her whereever she passed, was her air of radiant health and happiness, which emanated from her like the perfume from a flower.

A sad countenance may render a heroine of romance attractive in a book, but in real life there is no charm at once so rare and so fascinating as happiness. Did you ever think how few faces of the grown up, however young, are really happy in expression? Discontent, restlessness, longing, unsatisfied ambition or ill health mar ninety and nine of every hundred faces we meet in the daily walks of life. When we look upon a countenance which sparkles with health and absolute joy in life, we turn and look again and yet again, charmed and fascinated, though we do not know why.

It was such a face that Joy Irving, the new organist of St Blank's Church, flashed upon the people who had lingered near the door to see her pass out. Among those who lingered was the Baroness; and all day she carried about with her the memory of that sparkling countenance; and strive as she would, she could not drive away a vague, strange uneasiness which the sight of that face had caused her.

Yet a vision of youth and beauty always made the Baroness unhappy, now that both blessings were irrevocably lost to her.

This particular young face, however, stirred her with those half- painful, half-pleasurable emotions which certain perfumes awake in us--vague reminders of joys lost or unattained, of dreams broken or unrealised. Added to this, it reminded her of someone she had known, yet she could not place the resemblance.

"Oh, to be young and beautiful like that!" she sighed as she buried her face in her pillow that night. "And since I cannot be, if only Alice had that girl's face."

And because Alice did not have it, the Baroness went to sleep with a feeling of bitter resentment against its possessor, the beautiful young organist of St Blank's.

CHAPTER IX

Up in the loft of St Blank's Church the young organist had been practising the whole morning. People paused on the street to listen to the glorious sounds, and were thrilled by them, as one is only thrilled when the strong personality of the player enters into the execution.

Down into the committee-room, where several deacons and the young rector were seated discussing some question pertaining to the well- being of the church, the music penetrated too, causing the business which had brought them together, to be suspended temporarily.

"It is a sin to talk while music like that can be heard," remarked one man. "You have found a genius in this new organist, Rector."

The young man nodded silently, his eyes half closed with an expression of somewhat sensuous enjoyment of the throbbing chords which vibrated in perfect unison with the beating of his strong pulses.

"Where does she come from?" asked the deacon, as a pause in the music occurred.

"Her father was an earnest and prominent member of the little church downtown of which I had charge during several years," replied the young man. "Miss Irving was scarcely more than a child when she volunteered her services as organist. The position brought her no remuneration, and at that time she did not need it. Young as she was, the girl was one of the most active workers among the poor, and I often met her in my visits to the sick and unfortunate. She had been a musical prodigy from the cradle, and Mr Irving had given her every advantage to study and perfect her art.

"I was naturally much interested in her. Mr Irving's long illness left his wife and daughter without means of support, at his death, and when I was called to take charge of St Blank's, I at once realised the benefit to the family as well as to my church could I secure the young lady the position here as organist. I am glad that my congregation seem so well satisfied with my choice."

Again the organ pealed forth, this time in that passionate music originally written for the Garden Scene in Faust, and which the church has boldly taken and arranged as a quartette to the words, "Come unto me."

It may be that to some who listen, it is the divine spirit which makes its appeal through those stirring strains; but to the rector of St Blank's, at least on that morning, it was human heart, calling unto human heart. Mr Stuart and the deacons sat silently drinking in the music. At length the rector rose. "I think perhaps we had better drop the matter under discussion for to-day," he said. "We can meet here Monday evening at five o'clock if agreeable to you all, and finish the details. There are other and more important affairs waiting for me now."

The deacons departed, and the young rector sank back in his chair, and gave himself up to the enjoyment of the sounds which flooded not only the room, but his brain, heart and soul.

"Queer," he said to himself as the door closed behind the human pillars of his church. "Queer, but I felt as if the presence of those men was an intrusion upon something belonging personally to me. I wonder why I am so peculiarly affected by this girl's music? It arouses my brain to action, it awakens ambition and gives me courage and hope, and yet--" He paused before allowing his feeling to shape itself into thoughts. Then closing his eyes and clasping his hands behind his head while the music surged about him, he lay back in his easy-chair as a bather might lie back and float upon the water, and his unfinished sentence took shape thus: "And yet stronger than all other feelings which her music arouses in me, is the desire to possess the musician for my very own for ever; ah, well! the Roman Catholics are wise in not allowing their priests and their nuns to listen to all even so-called sacred music."

It was perhaps ten minutes later that Joy Irving became conscious that she was not alone in the organ loft. She had neither heard nor seen his entrance, but she felt the presence of her rector, and turned to find him silently watching her. She played her phrase to the end, before she greeted him with other than a smile. Then she apologised, saying: "Even one's rector must wait for a musical phrase to reach its period. Angels may interrupt the rendition of a great work, but not man. That were sacrilege. You see, I was really praying, when you entered, though my heart spoke through my fingers instead of my lips."

"You need not apologise," the young man answered. "One who receives your smile would be ungrateful indeed if he asked for more. That alone would render the darkest spot radiant with light and welcome to me."

The girl's pink cheek flushed crimson, like a rose bathed in the sunset colours of the sky.

"I did not think you were a man to coin pretty speeches," she said.

"Your estimate of me was a wise one. You read human nature correctly. But come and walk in the park with me. You will overtax yourself if you practise any longer. The sunlight and the air are vying with each other to-day to see which can be the most intoxicating. Come and enjoy their sparring match with me; I want to talk to you about one of my unfortunate parishioners. It is a peculiarly pathetic case. I think you can help and advise me in the matter."

It was a superb morning in early October. New York was like a beautiful woman arrayed in her fresh autumn costume, disporting herself before admiring eyes.

Absorbed in each other's society, their pulses beating high with youth, love and health; the young couple walked through the crowded avenues of the great city, as happily and as naturally as Adam and Eve might have walked in the Garden of Eden the morning after Creation.

Both were city born and city bred, yet both were as unfashionable and untrammelled by custom as two children of the plains.

In the very heart of the greatest metropolis in America, there are people who live and retain all the primitive simplicity of village life and thought. Mr Irving had been one of these. Coming to New York from an interior village when a young man, he had, through simple and quiet tastes and religious convictions, kept himself wholly free from the social life of the city in which he lived. After his marriage his entire happiness lay in his home, and Joy was reared by parents who made her world. Mrs Irving sympathised fully with her husband in his distaste for society, and her delicate health rendered her almost a recluse from the world.

A few pleasant acquaintances, no intimates, music, books, and a large share of her time given to charitable work, composed the life of Joy Irving.

She had never been in a fashionable assemblage; she had never attended a theatre, as Mr Irving did not approve of them.

Extremely fond of outdoor life, she walked, unattended, wherever her mood led her. As she had no acquaintances among society people, she knew nothing and cared less for the rules which govern the promenading habits of young women in New York. Her sweet face and graceful figure were well known among the poorer quarters of the city, and it was through her work in such places that Arthur Stuart's attention had first been called to her.

As for him, he was filled with that high, but not always wise, disdain for society and its customs, which we so often find in town- bred young men of intellectual pursuits. He was clean-minded, independent, sure of his own purposes, and wholly indifferent to the opinions of inferiors regarding his habits.

He loved the park, and he asked Joy to walk with him there, as freely as he would have asked her to sit with him in a conservatory. It was a great delight to the young girl to go.

"It seems such a pity that the women of New York get so little benefit from this beautiful park," she said as they strolled along through the winding paths together. "The wealthy people enjoy it in a way from their carriages, and the poor people no doubt derive new life from their Sunday promenades here. But there are thousands like myself who are almost wholly debarred from its pleasures. I have always wanted to walk here, but once I came and a rude man in a carriage spoke to me. Mother told me never to come alone again. It seems strange to me that men who are so proud of their strength, and who should be the natural protectors of woman, can belittle themselves by annoying or frightening her when alone. I am sure that same man would never think of speaking to me now that I am with you. How cowardly he seems when you think of it! Yet I am told there are many like him, though that was my only experience of the kind."

"Yes, there are many like him," the rector answered. "But you must remember how short a time man has been evolving from a lower animal condition to his present state, and how much higher he is to-day than he was a hundred years ago even, when occasional drunkenness was considered an attribute of a gentleman. Now it is a vice of which he is ashamed."

"Then you believe in evolution?" Joy asked with a note of surprise in her voice.

"Yes, I surely do; nor does the belief conflict with my religious faith. I believe in many things I could not preach from my pulpit. My congregation is not ready for broad truths. I am like an eclectic physician--I suit my treatment to my patient--I administer the old school or the new school medicaments as the case demands."

"It seems to me there can be but one school in spiritual matters," Joy said gravely--"the right one. And I think one should preach and teach what he believes to be true and right, no matter what his congregation demands. Oh, forgive me. I am very rude to speak like that to you!" And she blushed and paled with fright at her boldness.

They were seated on a rustic bench now, under the shadow of a great tree.

The rector smiled, his eyes fixed with pleased satisfaction on the girl's beautiful face, with its changing colour and expression. He felt he could well afford to be criticised or rebuked by her, if the result was so gratifying to his sight. The young rector of St Blank's lived very much more in his senses than in his ideals.

"Perhaps you are right," he said. "I sometimes wish I had greater courage of my convictions. I think I could have, were you to stimulate me with such words often. But my mother is so afraid that I will wander from the old dogmas, that I am constantly checking myself. However, in regard to the case I mentioned to you--it is a delicate subject, but you are not like ordinary young women, and you and I have stood beside so many sick-beds and death-beds together that we can speak as man to man, or woman to woman, with no false modesty to bar our speech.

"A very sad case has come to my knowledge of late. Miss Adams, a woman who for some years has been a devout member of St Blank's Church, has several times mentioned her niece to me, a young girl who was away at boarding school. A few months ago the young girl graduated and came to live with this aunt. I remember her as a bright, buoyant and very intelligent girl. I have not seen her now during two months; and last week I asked Miss Adams what had become of her niece. Then the poor woman broke into sobs and told me the sad state of affairs. It seems that the girl Marah is her daughter. The poor mother had believed she could guard the truth from her child, and had educated her as her niece, and was now prepared to enjoy her companionship, when some mischief-making gossip dug up the old scandal and imparted the facts to Marah.

"The girl came to Miss Adams and demanded the truth, and the mother confessed. Then the daughter settled into a profound melancholy, from which nothing seemed to rouse her. She will not go out, remains in the house, and broods constantly over her disgrace.

"It occurred to me that if Marah Adams could be brought out of herself and interested in some work, or study, it would be the salvation of her reason. Her mother told me she is an accomplished musician, but that she refuses to touch her piano now. I thought you might take her as an understudy on the organ, and by your influence and association lead her out of herself. You could make her acquaintance through approaching the mother who is a milliner, on business, and your tact would do the rest. In all my large and wealthy congregation I know of no other woman to whom I could appeal for aid in this delicate matter, so I am sure you will pardon me. In fact, I fear were the matter to be known in the congregation at all, it would lead to renewed pain and added hurts for both Miss Adams and her daughter. You know women can be so cruel to each other in subtle ways, and I have seen almost death-blows dealt in church aisles by one church member to another."

"Oh, that is a terrible reflection on Christians," cried Joy, who, a born Christ-woman, believed that all professed church members must feel the same divine spirit of sympathy and charity which burned in her own sweet soul.

"No, it is a simple truth--an unfortunate fact," the young man replied. "I preach sermons at such members of my church, but they seldom take them home. They think I mean somebody else. These are the people who follow the letter and not the spirit of the church. But one such member as you, recompenses me for a score of the others. I felt I must come to you with the Marah Adams affair."

Joy was still thinking of the reflection the rector had cast upon his congregation. It hurt her, and she protested.

"Oh, surely," she said, "you cannot mean that I am the only one of the professed Christians in your church who would show mercy and sympathy to poor Miss Adams. Surely few, very few, would forget Christ's words to Mary Magdalene, 'Go and sin no more,' or fail to forgive as He forgave. She has led such a good life all these years."

The rector smiled sadly.

"You judge others by your own true heart," he said. "But I know the world as it is. Yes, the members of my church would forgive Miss Adams for her sin--and cut her dead. They would daily crucify her and her innocent child by their cold scorn or utter ignoring of them. They would not allow their daughters to associate with this blameless girl, because of her mother's misstep.

"It is the same in and out of the churches. Twenty people will repeat Christ's words to a repentant sinner, but nineteen of that twenty interpolate a few words of their own, through tone, gesture or manner, until 'Go and sin no more' sounds to the poor unfortunate more like 'Go just as far away from me and mine as you can get--and sin no more!' Only one in that score puts Christ's merciful and tender meaning into the phrase and tries by sympathetic association to make it possible for the sinner to sin no more. I felt you were that one, and so I appealed to you in this matter about Marah Adams."

Joy's eyes were full of tears. "You must know more of human nature than I do," she said, "but I hate terribly to think you are right in this estimate of the people of your congregation. I will go and see what I can do for this girl to-morrow. Poor child, poor mother, to pass through a second Gethsemane for her sin. I think any girl or boy whose home life is shadowed, is to be pitied. I have always had such a happy home, and such dear parents, the world would seem insupportable, I am sure, were I to face it without that background. Dear papa's death was a great blow, and mother's ill health has been a sorrow, but we have always been so happy and harmonious, and that, I think, is worth more than a fortune to a child. Poor, poor Marah-- unable to respect her mother, what a terrible thing it all is!"

"Yes, it is a sad affair. I cannot help thinking it would have been a pardonable lie if Miss Adams had denied the truth when the girl confronted her with the story. It is the one situation in life where a lie is excusable, I think. It would have saved this poor girl no end of sorrow, and it could not have added much to the mother's burden. I think lying must have originated with an erring woman."

Joy looked at her rector with startled eyes. "A lie is never excusable," she said, "and I do not believe it ever saves sorrow. But I see you do not mean what you say, you only feel very sorry for the girl; and you surely do not forget that the lie originated with Satan, who told a falsehood to Eve."

CHAPTER X

Ever since early girlhood Joy Irving had formed a habit of jotting down in black and white her own ideas regarding any book, painting, concert, conversation or sermon, which interested her, and epitomising the train of thought to which they led.

The evening after her walk and talk with the rector of St Blank's, she took out her note-book, which bore a date four years old under its title "My Impressions," and read over the last page of entries. They had evidently been written at the close of some Sabbath day and ran as follows:-

Many a kneeling woman is more occupied with how her skirts hang than how her prayers ascend. I am inclined to think we all ought to wear a uniform to church if we would really worship there. God must grow weary looking down on so many new bonnets.

I wore a smart hat to church to-day, and I found myself criticising every other woman's bonnet during service, so that I failed in some of my responses.

If we could all be compelled by some mysterious power to THINK ALOUD on Sunday, what a veritable holy day we would make of it! Though we are taught from childhood that God hears our thoughts, the best of us would be afraid to have our nearest friends know them.

I sometimes think it is a presumption on the part of any man to rise in the pulpit and undertake to tell me about a Creator with whom I feel every whit as well acquainted as he. I suppose such thoughts are wicked, however, and should be suppressed.

It is a curious fact, that the most aggressively sensitive persons are at heart the most conceited.

I wish people smiled more in church aisles. In fact, I think we all laugh at one another too much and smile at one another too seldom.

After the devil had made all the trouble for woman he could with the fig leaf, he introduced the French heel.

It is well to see the ridiculous side of things, but not of people.

Most of us would rather be popular than right.

To these impressions Joy added the following:-

It is not the interior of one's house, but the interior of one's mind which makes home.

It seems to me that to be, is to love. I can conceive of no state of existence which is not permeated with this feeling toward something, somebody or the illimitable "nothing" which is mother to everything.

I wish we had more religion in the world and fewer churches.

People who believe in no God, invariably exalt themselves into His position, and worship with the very idolatry they decry in others.

Music is the echo of the rhythm of God's respirations.

Poetry is the effort of the divine part of man to formulate a worthy language in which to converse with angels.

Painting and sculpture seem to me the most presumptuous of the arts. They are an effort of man to outdo God in creation. He never made a perfect form or face-- the artist alone makes them.

I am sure I do not play the organ as well at St Blank's as I played it in the little church where I gave my services and was unknown. People are praising me too much here, and this mars all spontaneity.

The very first hour of positive success is often the last hour of great achievement. So soon as we are conscious of the admiring and expectant gaze of men, we cease to commune with God. It is when we are unknown to or neglected by mortals, that we reach up to the Infinite and are inspired.

I have seen Marah Adams to-day, and I felt strangely drawn to her. Her face would express all goodness if it were not so unhappy. Unhappiness is a species of evil, since it is a discourtesy to God to be unhappy.

I am going to do all I can for the girl to bring her into a better frame of mind. No blame can be attached to her, and yet now that I am face to face with the situation, and realise how the world regards such a person, I myself find it a little hard to think of braving public opinion and identifying myself with her. But I am going to overcome such feelings, as they are cowardly and unworthy of me, and purely the result of education. I am amazed, too, to discover this weakness in myself.

How sympathetic dear mamma is! I told her about Marah, and she wept bitterly, and has carried her eyes full of tears ever since. I must be careful and tell her nothing sad while she is in such a weak state physically.

I told mamma what the rector said about lying. She coincided with him that Mrs Adams would have been justified in denying the truth if she had realised how her daughter was to be affected by this knowledge. A woman's past belongs only to herself and her God, she says, unless she wishes to make a confidant. But I cannot agree with her or the rector. I would want the truth from my parents, however much it hurt. Many sins which men regard as serious only obstruct the bridge between our souls and truth. A lie burns the bridge.

I hope I am not uncharitable, yet I cannot conceive of committing an act through love of any man, which would lower me in his esteem, once committed. Yet of course I have had little experience in life, with men, or with temptation. But it seems to me I could not continue to love a man who did not seek to lead me higher. The moment he stood before me and asked me to descend, I should realise he was to be pitied--not adored.

I told mother this, and she said I was too young and inexperienced to form decided opinions on such subjects, and she warned me that I must not become uncharitable. She wept bitterly as she thought of my becoming narrow or bigoted in my ideas, dear, tender-hearted mamma.

Death should be called the Great Revealer instead of the Great Destroyer.

Some people think the way into heaven is through embroidered altar cloths.

The soul that has any conception of its own possibilities does not fear solitude.

A girl told me to-day that a rude man annoyed her by staring at her in a public conveyance. It never occurred to her that it takes four eyes to make a stare annoying.

Astronomers know more about the character of the stars than the average American mother knows about the temperament of her daughters.

To some women the most terrible thought connected with death is the dates in the obituary notice.

As a rule, when a woman opens the door of an artistic career with one hand, she shuts the door on domestic happiness with the other.

CHAPTER XI

The rector of St Blank's Church dined at the Cheney table or drove in the Cheney establishment every week, beside which there were always one or two confidential chats with the feminine Cheneys in the parsonage on matters pertaining to the welfare of the church, and occasionally to the welfare of humanity.

That Alice Cheney had conceived a sudden and consuming passion for the handsome and brilliant rector of St Blank's, both her mother and the Baroness knew, and both were doing all in their power to further the girl's hopes.

While Alice resembled her mother in appearance and disposition, propensities and impulses occasionally exhibited themselves which spoke of paternal inheritance. She had her father's strongly emotional nature, with her mother's stubbornness; and Preston Cheney's romantic tendencies were repeated in his daughter, without his reasoning powers. Added to her father's lack of self-control in any strife with his passions, Alice possessed her mother's hysterical nerves. In fact, the unfortunate child inherited the weaknesses and faults of both parents, without any of their redeeming virtues.

The passion which had sprung to life in her breast for the young rector, was as strong and unreasoning as the infatuation which her father had once experienced for Berene Dumont; but instead of struggling against the feeling as her father had at least attempted to do, she dwelt upon it with all the mulish persistency which her mother exhibited in small matters, and luxuriated in romantic dreams of the future.

Mabel was wholly unable to comprehend the depth or violence of her daughter's feelings, but she realised the fact that Alice had set her mind on winning Arthur Stuart for a husband, and she quite approved of the idea, and saw no reason why it should not succeed. She herself had won Preston Cheney away from all rivals for his favour, and Alice ought to be able to do the same with Arthur, after all the money which had been expended upon her wardrobe. Senator Cheney's daughter and Judge Lawrence's granddaughter, surely was a prize for any man to win as a wife.

The Baroness, however, reviewed the situation with more concern of mind. She realised that Alice was destitute of beauty and charm, and that Arthur Emerson Stuart (it would have been considered a case of high treason to speak of the rector of St Blank's without using his three names) was independent in the matter of fortune, and so dowered with nature's best gifts that he could have almost any woman for the asking whom he should desire. But the Baroness believed much in propinquity; and she brought the rector and Alice together as often as possible, and coached the girl in coquettish arts when alone with her, and credited her with witticisms and bon-mots which she had never uttered, when talking of her to the young rector.

"If only I could give Alice the benefit of my past career," the Baroness would say to herself at times. "I know so well how to manage men; but what use is my knowledge to me now that I am old? Alice is young, and even without beauty she could do so much, if she only understood the art of masculine seduction. But then it is a gift, not an acquired art, and Alice was not born with the gift."

While Mabel and Alice had been centring their thoughts and attentions on the rector, the Baroness had not forgotten the rector's mother. She knew the very strong affection which existed between the two, and she had discovered that the leading desire of the young man's heart was to make his mother happy. With her wide knowledge of human nature, she had not been long in discerning the fact that it was not because of his own religious convictions that the rector had chosen his calling, but to carry out the lifelong wishes of his beloved mother.

Therefore she reasoned wisely that Arthur would be greatly influenced by his mother in his choice of a wife; and the Baroness brought all her vast battery of fascination to bear on Mrs Stuart, and succeeded in making that lady her devoted friend.

The widow of Judge Lawrence was still an imposing and impressive figure wherever she went. Though no longer a woman who appealed to the desires of men, she exhaled that peculiar mental aroma which hangs ever about a woman who has dealt deeply and widely in affairs of the heart. It is to the spiritual senses what musk is to the physical; and while it may often repulse, it sometimes attracts, and never fails to be noticed. About the Baroness's mouth were hard lines, and the expression of her eyes was not kind or tender; yet she was everywhere conceded to be a universally handsome and attractive woman. Quiet and tasteful in her dressing, she did not accentuate the ravages of time by any mistaken frivolities of toilet, as so many faded coquettes have done, but wisely suited her vestments to her appearance, as the withering branch clothes itself in russet leaves, when the fresh sap ceases to course through its veins. New York City is a vast sepulchre of "past careers," and the adventurous life of the Baroness was quietly buried there with that of many another woman. In the mad whirl of life there is small danger that any of these skeletons will rise to view, unless the woman permits herself to strive for eminence either socially or in the world of art.

While the Cheneys were known to be wealthy, and the Senator had achieved political position, there was nothing in their situation to challenge the jealousy of their associates. They moved in one of the many circles of cultured and agreeable people, which, despite the mandate of a M'Allister, formed a varied and delightful society in the metropolis; they entertained in an unostentatious manner, and there was nothing in their personality to incite envy or jealousy. Therefore the career of the Baroness had not been unearthed. That the widow of Judge Lawrence, the stepmother of Mrs Cheney, was known as "The Baroness" caused some questions, to be sure, but the simple answer that she had been the widow of a French baron in early life served to allay curiosity, while it rendered the lady herself an object of greater interest to the majority of people.

Mrs Stuart, the rector's mother, was one of those who were most impressed by this incident in the life of Mrs Lawrence. "Family pride" was her greatest weakness, and she dearly loved a title. She thought Mrs Lawrence a typical "Baroness," and though she knew the title had only been obtained through marriage, it still rendered its possessor peculiarly interesting in her eyes.

In her prime, the Baroness had been equally successful in cajoling women and men. Though her day for ruling men was now over, she still possessed the power to fascinate women when she chose to exert herself. She did exert herself with Mrs Stuart, and succeeded admirably in her design.

And one day Mrs Stuart confided her secret anxiety to the ear of the Baroness; and that secret caused the cheek of the listener to grow pale and the look of an animal at bay to come into her eyes.

"There is just one thing that gives me a constant pain at my heart," Mrs Stuart had said. "You have never been a mother, yet I think your sympathetic nature causes you to understand much which you have not experienced, and knowing as you do the great pride I feel in my son's career, and the ambition I have for him to rise to the very highest pinnacle of success and usefulness, I am sure you will comprehend my anxiety when I see him exhibiting an undue interest in a girl who is in every way his inferior, and wholly unsuited to fill the position his wife should occupy."

The Baroness listened with a cold, sinking sensation at her heart

"I am sure your son would never make a choice which was not agreeable to you," she ventured.

"He might not marry anyone I objected to," Mrs Stuart replied, "but I dread to think his heart may be already gone from his keeping. Young men are so susceptible to a pretty face and figure, and I confess that Joy Irving has both. She is a good girl, too, and a fine musician; but she has no family, and her alliance with my son would be a great drawback to his career. Her father was a grocer, I believe, or something of that sort; quite a common man, who married a third-class actress, Joy's mother. Mr Irving was in very comfortable circumstances at one time, but a stroke of paralysis rendered him helpless some four years ago. He died last year and left his widow and child in straitened circumstances. Mrs Irving is an invalid now, and Joy supports her with her music. Mr Irving and Joy were members of Arthur Emerson's former church (Mrs Stuart always spoke of her son in that manner), and that is how my son became interested in the daughter--an interest I supposed to be purely that of a rector in his parishioner, until of late, when I began to fear it took root in deeper soil. But I am sure, dear Baroness, you can understand my anxiety."

And then the Baroness, with drawn lips and anguished eyes, took both of Mrs Stuart's hands in hers, and cried out:

"Your pain, dear madam, is second to mine. I have no child, to be sure, but as few mothers love I love Alice Cheney, my dear husband's granddaughter. My very life is bound up in her, and she--God help us, she loves your son with her whole soul. If he marries another it will kill her or drive her insane."

The two women fell weeping into each other's arms.

CHAPTER XII

Preston Cheney conceived such a strong, earnest liking for the young clergyman whom he met under his own roof during one of his visits home, that he fell into the habit of attending church for the first time in his life.

Mabel and Alice were deeply gratified with this intimacy between the two men, which brought the rector to the house far oftener than they could have tastefully done without the co-operation of the husband and father. Besides, it looked well to have the head of the household represented in the church. To the Baroness, also, there was added satisfaction in attending divine service, now that Preston Cheney sat in the pew. All hope of winning the love she had so longed to possess, died many years before; and she had been cruel and unkind in numerous ways to the object of her hopeless passion, yet like the smell of dead rose leaves long shut in a drawer, there clung about this man the faint, suggestive fragrance of a perished dream.

She knew that he did not love his wife, and that he was disappointed in his daughter; and she did not at least have to suffer the pain of seeing him lavish the affection she had missed, on others.

Mr Cheney had been called away from home on business the day before the new organist took her place in St Blank's Church. Nearly a month had passed when he again occupied his pew.

Before the organist had finished her introduction, he turned to Alice, saying:

"There has been a change here in the choir, since I went away, and for the better. That is a very unusual musician. Do you know who it is?"

"Some lady, I believe; I do not remember her name," Alice answered indifferently. Like her mother, Alice never enjoyed hearing anyone praised. It mattered little who it was, or how entirely out of her own line the achievements or accomplishments on which the praise was bestowed, she still felt that petty resentment of small creatures who believe that praise to others detracts from their own value.

A fortune had been expended on Alice's musical education, yet she could do no more than rattle through some mediocre composition, with neither taste nor skill.

The money which has been wasted in trying to teach music to unmusical people would pay our national debt twice over, and leave a competency for every orphan in the land.

When the organist had finished her second selection, Mr Cheney addressed the same question to his wife which he had addressed to Alice.

"Who is the new organist?" he queried. Mabel only shook her head and placed her finger on her lip as a signal for silence during service.

The third time it was the Baroness, sitting just beyond Mabel, to whom Mr Cheney spoke. "That's a very remarkable musician, very remarkable," he said. "Do you know anything about her?"

"Yes, wait until we get home, and I will tell you all about her," the Baroness replied.

When the service was over, Mr Cheney did not pass out at once, as was his custom. Instead he walked toward the pulpit, after requesting his family to wait a moment.

The rector saw him and came down into the aisle to speak to him.

"I want to congratulate you on the new organist," Mr Cheney said, "and I want to meet her. Alice tells me it is a lady. She must have devoted a lifetime to hard study to become such a marvellous mistress of that difficult instrument."

Arthur Stuart smiled. "Wait a moment," he said, "and I will send for her. I would like you to meet her, and like her to meet your wife and family. She has few, if any, acquaintances in my congregation."

Mr Cheney went down the aisle, and joined the three ladies who were waiting for him in the pew. All were smiling, for all three believed that he had been asking the rector to accompany them home to dinner. His first word dispelled the illusion.

"Wait here a moment," he said. "Mr Stuart is going to bring the organist to meet us. I want to know the woman who can move me so deeply by her music."

Over the faces of his three listeners there fell a cloud. Mabel looked annoyed,

Alice sulky, and a flush of the old jealous fury darkened the brow of the Baroness. But all were smiling deceitfully when Joy Irving approached.

Her radiant young beauty, and the expressions of admiration with which Preston Cheney greeted her as a woman and an artist, filled life with gall and wormwood for the three feminine listeners.

"What! this beautiful young miss, scarcely out of short frocks, is not the musician who gave us that wonderful harmony of sounds. My child, how did you learn to play like that in the brief life you have passed on earth? Surely you must have been taught by the angels before you came."

A deep blush of pleasure at the words which, though so extravagant, Joy felt to be sincere, increased her beauty as she looked up into Preston Cheney's admiring eyes.

And as he held her hands in both of his and gazed down upon her it seemed to the Baroness she could strike them dead at her feet and rejoice in the act.

Beside this radiant vision of loveliness and genius, Alice looked plainer and more meagre than ever before. She was like a wayside weed beside an American Beauty rose.

"I hope you and Alice will become good friends," Mr Cheney said warmly. "We should like to see you at the house any time you can make it convenient to come, would we not Mabel?"

Mrs Cheney gave a formal assent to her husband's words as they turned away, leaving Joy with the rector. And a scene in one of life's strangest dramas had been enacted, unknown to them all.

"I would like you to be very friendly with that girl, Alice," Mr Cheney repeated as they seated themselves in the carriage. "She has a rare face, a rare face, and she is highly gifted. She reminds me of someone I have known, yet I can't think who it is. What do you know about her, Baroness?"

The Baroness gave an expressive shrug. "Since you admire her so much," she said, "I rather hesitate telling you. But the girl is of common origin--a grocer's daughter, and her mother quite an inferior person. I hardly think it a suitable companionship for Alice."

"I am sure I don't care to know her," chimed in Alice. "I thought her quite bold and forward in her manner."

"Decidedly so! She seemed to hang on to your father's hand as if she would never let go," added Mabel, in her most acid tone. "I must say, I should have been horrified to see you act in such a familiar manner toward any stranger." A quick colour shot into Preston Cheney's cheek and a spark into his eye.

"The girl was perfectly modest in her deportment to me," he said. "She is a lady through and through, however humble her birth may be. But I ought to have known better than to ask my wife and daughter to like anyone whom I chanced to admire. I learned long ago how futile such an idea was."

"Oh, well, I don't see why you need get so angry over a perfect stranger whom you never laid eyes on until to-day," pouted Alice. "I am sure she's nothing to any of us that we need quarrel over her."

"A man never gets so old that he is not likely to make a fool of himself over a pretty face," supplemented Mabel, "and there is no fool like an old fool."

The uncomfortable drive home came to an end at this juncture, and Preston Cheney retired to his own room, with the disagreeable words of his wife and daughter ringing in his ears, and the beautiful face of the young organist floating before his eyes.

"I wish she were my daughter," he said to himself; "what a comfort and delight a girl like that would be to me!"

And while these thoughts filled the man's heart the Baroness paced her room with all the jealous passions of her still ungoverned nature roused into new life and violence at the remembrance of Joy Irving's fresh young beauty and Preston Cheney's admiring looks and words.

"I could throttle her," she cried, "I could throttle her. Oh, why is she sent across my life at every turn? Why should the only two men in the world who interest me to-day, be so infatuated over that girl? But if I cannot remove so humble an obstacle as she from my pathway, I shall feel that my day of power is indeed over, and that I do not believe to be true."

CHAPTER XIII

Two weeks later the organ loft of St Blank's Church was occupied by a stranger. For a few hours the Baroness felt a wild hope in her heart that Miss Irving had been sent away.

But inquiry elicited the information that the young musician had merely employed a substitute because her mother was lying seriously ill at home.

It was then that the Baroness put into execution a desire she had to make the personal acquaintance of Joy Irving.

The desire had sprung into life with the knowledge of the rector's interest in the girl. No one knew better than the Baroness how to sow the seeds of doubt, distrust and discord between two people whom she wished to alienate. Many a sweetheart, many a wife, had she separated from lover and husband, scarcely leaving a sign by which the trouble could be traced to her, so adroit and subtle were her methods.

She felt that she could insert an invisible wedge between these two hearts, which would eventually separate them, if only she might make the acquaintance of Miss Irving. And now chance had opened the way for her.

She made her resolve known to the rector.

"I am deeply interested in the young organist whom I had the pleasure of meeting some weeks ago," she said, and she noted with a sinking heart the light which flashed into the man's face at the mere mention of the girl. "I understand her mother is seriously ill, and I think I will go around and call. Perhaps I can be of use. I understand Mrs Irving is not a churchwoman, and she may be in real need, as the family is in straitened circumstances. May I mention your name when I call, in order that Miss Irving may not think I intrude?"

"Why, certainly," the rector replied with warmth. "Indeed, I will give you a card of introduction. That will open the way for you, and at the same time I know you will use your delicate tact to avoid wounding Miss Irving's pride in any way. She is very sensitive about their straitened circumstances; you may have heard that they were quite well-to-do until the stroke of paralysis rendered her father helpless. All their means were exhausted in efforts to restore his health, and in the employment of nurses and physicians. I think they have found life a difficult problem since his death, as Mrs Irving has been under medical care constantly, and the whole burden falls on Miss Joy's young shoulders, and she is but twenty-one."

"Just the age of Alice," mused the Baroness. "How differently people's lives are ordered in this world! But then we must have the hewers of wood and the drawers of water, and we must have the delicate human flowers. Our Alice is one of the latter, a frail blossom to look upon, but she is one of the kind which will bloom out in great splendour under the sunshine of love and happiness. Very few people realise what wonderful reserve force that delicate child possesses. And such a tender heart! She was determined to come with me when she heard of Miss Irving's trouble, but I thought it unwise to take her until I had seen the place. She is so sensitive to her surroundings, and it might be too painful for her. I am for ever holding her back from overtaxing herself for others. No one dreams of the amount of good that girl does in a secret, quiet way; and at the same time she assumes an indifferent air and talks as if she were quite heartless, just to hinder people from suspecting her charitable work. She is such a strange, complicated character."

Armed with her card of introduction, the Baroness set forth on her "errand of mercy." She had not mentioned Miss Irving's name to Mabel or Alice. The secret of the rector's interest in the girl was locked in her own breast. She knew that Mabel was wholly incapable of coping with such a situation, and she dreaded the effect of the news on Alice, who was absorbed in her love dream. The girl had never been denied a wish in her life, and no thought came to her that she could be thwarted in this, her most cherished hope of all.

The Baroness was determined to use every gun in her battery of defence before she allowed Mabel or Alice to know that defence was needed.

The rector's card admitted her to the parlour of a small flat. The portieres of an adjoining room were thrown open presently, and a vision of radiant beauty entered the room.

The Baroness could not explain it, but as the girl emerged from the curtains, a strange, confused memory of something and somebody she had known in the past came over her. But when the girl spoke, a more inexplicable sensation took possession of the listener, for her voice was the feminine of Preston Cheney's masculine tones, and then as she looked at the girl again the haunting memories of the first glance were explained, for she was very like Preston Cheney as the Baroness remembered him when he came to the Palace to engage rooms more than a score of years ago. "What a strange thing these resemblances are!" she thought. "This girl is more like Senator Cheney, far more like him, than Alice is. Ah, if Alice only had her face and form!"

Miss Irving gave a slight start, and took a step back as her eyes fell upon the Baroness. The rector's card had read, "Introducing Mrs Sylvester Lawrence." She had known this lad by sight ever since her first Sunday as organist at St Blank's, and for some unaccountable reason she had conceived a most intense dislike for her. Joy was drawn toward humanity in general, as naturally as the sunlight falls on the earth's foliage. Her heart radiated love and sympathy toward the whole world. But when she did feel a sentiment of distrust or repulsion she had learned to respect it.

Our guardian angels sometimes send these feelings as danger signals to our souls.

It therefore required a strong effort of her will to go forward and extend a hand in greeting to the lady whom her rector and friend had introduced.

"I must beg pardon for this intrusion," the Baroness said with her sweetest smile; "but our rector urged me to come and so I felt emboldened to carry out the wish I have long entertained to make your acquaintance. Your wonderful music inspires all who hear you to know you personally; the service lacked half its charm on Sunday because you were absent. When I learnt that your absence was occasioned by your mother's illness, I asked the rector if he thought a call from me would be an intrusion, and he assured me to the contrary. I used to be considered an excellent nurse; I am very strong, and full of vitality, and if you would permit me to sit by your mother some Sunday when you are needed at church, I should be most happy to do so. I should like to make the acquaintance of your mother, and compliment her on the happiness of possessing such a gifted and dutiful daughter."

Like all who sat for any time under the spell of the second Mrs Lawrence, Joy felt the charm of her voice, words and manner, and it began to seem as if she had been very unreasonable in entertaining unfounded prejudices.

That the rector had introduced her was alone proof of her worthiness; and the gracious offer of the distinguished-looking lady to watch by the bedside of a stranger was certainly evidence of her good heart. The frost disappeared from her smile, and she warmed toward the Baroness. The call lengthened into a visit, and as the Baroness finally rose to go, Joy said:

"I will take you in and introduce you to mamma now. I think it will do her good to meet you," and the Baroness followed the graceful girl through a narrow hall, and into a room which had evidently been intended for a dining-room, but which, owing to its size and its windows opening to the south, had been utilised as a sick chamber.

The invalid lay with her face turned away from the door. But by the movement of the delicate hand on the counterpane, Joy knew that her mother was awake.

"Mamma, I have brought a lady, a friend of Dr Stuart's, to see you," Joy said gently. The invalid turned her head upon the pillow, and the Baroness looked upon the face of--Berene Dumont.

"Berene!"

"Madam!"

The two spoke simultaneously, and the invalid had started upright in bed.

"Mamma, what is the matter? Oh, please lie down, or you will bring on another haemorrhage," cried the startled girl; but her mother lifted her hand.

"Joy," she said in a firm, clear voice, "this lady is an old acquaintance of mine. Please go out, dear, and shut the door. I wish to see her alone."

Joy passed out with drooping head and a sinking heart. As the door closed behind her the Baroness spoke.

"So that is Preston Cheney's daughter," she said. "I always had my suspicions of the cause which led you to leave my house so suddenly. Does the girl know who her father is? And does Senator Cheney know of her existence, may I ask?"

A crimson flush suffused the invalid's face. Then a flame of fire shot into the dark eyes, and a small red spot only glowed on either pale cheek.

"I do not know by what right you ask these questions, Baroness Brown," she answered slowly; and her listener cringed under the old appellation which recalled the miserable days when she had kept a lodging-house--days she had almost forgotten during the last decade of life.

"But I can assure you, madam," continued the speaker, "that my daughter knows no father save the good man, my husband, who is dead. I have never by word or line made my existence known to anyone I ever knew since I left Beryngford. I do not know why you should come here to insult me, madam; I have never harmed you or yours, and you have no proof of the accusation you just made, save your own evil suspicions."

The Baroness gave an unpleasant laugh.

"It is an easy matter for me to find proof of my suspicions if I choose to take the trouble," she said. "There are detectives enough to hunt up your trail, and I have money enough to pay them for their trouble. But Joy is the living evidence of the assertion. She is the image of Preston Cheney, as he was twenty-three years ago. I am ready, however, to let the matter drop on one condition; and that condition is, that you extract a promise from your daughter that she will not encourage the attentions of Arthur Emerson Stuart, the rector of St Blank's; that she will never under any circumstances be his wife."

The red spots faded to a sickly yellow in the invalid's cheeks. "Why should you ask this of me?" she cried. "Why should you wish to destroy the happiness of my child's life? She loves Arthur Stuart, and I know that he loves her! It is the one thought which resigns me to death; the thought that I may leave her the beloved wife of this good man."

The Baroness leaned lower over the pillow of the invalid as she answered: "I will tell you why I ask this sacrifice of you."

"Perhaps you do not know that I married Judge Lawrence after the death of his first wife. Perhaps you do not know that Preston Cheney's legitimate daughter is as precious to me as his illegitimate child is to you. Alice is only six months younger than Joy; she is frail, delicate, sensitive. A severe disappointment would kill her. She, too, loves Arthur Stuart. If your daughter will let him alone, he will marry Alice. Surely the illegitimate child should give way to the legitimate.

"If you are selfish in this matter, I shall be obliged to tell your daughter the true story of her life, and let her be the judge of what is right and what is wrong. I fancy she might have a finer perception of duty than you have--she is so much like her father."

The tortured invalid fell back panting on her pillow. She put out her hands with a distracted, imploring gesture.

"Leave me to think," she gasped. "I never knew that Preston Cheney had a daughter; I did not know he lived here. My life has been so quiet, so secluded these many years. Leave me to think. I will give you my answer in a few days; I will write you after I reflect and pray."

The Baroness passed out, and Joy, hastening into the room, found her mother in a wild paroxysm of tears. Late that night Mrs Irving called for writing materials; and for many hours she sat propped up in bed writing rapidly.

When she had completed her task she called Joy to her side.

"Darling," she said, placing a sealed manuscript in her hands, "I want you to keep this seal unbroken so long as you are happy. I know in spite of your deep sorrow at my death, which must come ere long, you will find much happiness in life. You came smiling into existence, and no common sorrow can deprive you of the joy which is your birthright. But there are numerous people in the world who may strive to wound you after I am gone. If slanderous tales or cruel reports reach your ears, and render you unhappy, break this seal, and read the story I have written here. There are some things which will deeply pain you, I know. Do not force yourself to read them until a necessity arises. I leave you this manuscript as I might leave you a weapon for self-defence. Use it only when you are in need of that defence."

The next morning Mrs Irving was weakened by another and most serious haemorrhage of the lungs. Her physician was grave, and urged the daughter to be prepared for the worst.

"I fear your mother's life is a matter of days only," he said.

CHAPTER XIV

The Baroness went directly from the home which she had entered only to blight, and sent her card marked "urgent" to Mrs Stuart.

"I have come to tell you an unpleasant story," she said--"a painful and revolting story, the early chapters of which were written years ago, but the sequel has only just been made known to me. It concerns you and yours vitally; it also concerns me and mine. I am sure, when you have heard the story to the end, you will say that truth is stranger than fiction, indeed: and you will more than ever realise the necessity of preventing your son from marrying Joy Irving--a child who was born before her mother ever met Mr Irving; and whose mother, I daresay, was no more the actual wife of Mr Irving in the name of law and decency than she had been the wife of his many predecessors."

Startled and horrified at this beginning of the story, Mrs Stuart was in a state of excited indignation at the end. The Baroness had magnified facts and distorted truths until she represented Berene Dumont as a monster of depravity; a vicious being who had been for a short time the recipient of the Baroness's mistaken charity, and who had repaid kindness by base ingratitude, and immorality. The man implicated in the scandal which she claimed was the cause of Berene's flight was not named in this recital.

Indeed the Baroness claimed that he was more sinned against than sinning, and that it was a case of mesmeric influence, or evil eye, on the part of the depraved woman.

Mrs Lawrence took pains to avoid any reference to Beryngford also; speaking of these occurrences having taken place while she spent a summer in a distant interior town, where, "after the death of the Baron, she had rented a villa, feeling that she wanted to retire from the world."

"My heart is always running away with my head," she remarked, "and I thought this poor creature, who was shunned and neglected by all, worth saving. I tried to befriend her, and hoped to waken the better nature which every woman possesses, I think, but she was too far gone in iniquity.

"You cannot imagine, my dear Mrs Stuart, what a shock it was to me on entering that sickroom to-day, my heart full of kindly sympathy, to encounter in the invalid the ungrateful recipient of my past favours; and to realise that her daughter was no other than the shameful offspring of her immoral past. In spite of the girl's beauty, there is an expression about her face which I never liked; and I fully understand now why I did not like it. Of course, Mrs Stuart, this story is told to you in strict confidence. I would not for the world have dear Mrs Cheney know of it, nor would I pollute sweet Alice with such a tale. Indeed, Alice would not understand it if she were told, for she is as ignorant and innocent as a child in arms of such matters. We have kept her absolutely unspotted from the world. But I knew it was my duty to tell you the whole shameful story. If worst comes to worst, you will be obliged to tell your son perhaps, and if he doubts the story send him to me for its verification."

Worst came to the worst before twenty-four hours had passed. The rector received word that Mrs Irving was rapidly failing, and went to act the part of spiritual counsellor to the invalid, and sympathetic friend to the suffering girl.

When he returned his mother watched his face with eager, anxious eyes. He looked haggard and ill, as if he had passed through a severe ordeal. He could talk of nothing but the beautiful and brave girl, who was about to lose her one worshipped companion, and who ere many hours passed would stand utterly alone in the world.

"I never saw you so affected before by the troubles and sorrows of your parishioners," Mrs Stuart said. "I wonder, Arthur, why you take the sorrows of this family so keenly to heart."

The young rector looked his mother full in the face with calm, sad eyes. Then he said slowly:

"I suppose, mother, it is because I love Joy Irving with all my heart. You must have suspected this for some time. I know that you have, and that the thought has pained you. You have had other and more ambitious aims for me. Earnest Christian and good woman that you are, you have a worldly and conventional vein in your nature, which makes you reverence position, wealth and family to a marked degree. You would, I know, like to see me unite myself with some royal family, were that possible; failing in that, you would choose the daughter of some great and aristocratic house to be my bride. Ah, well, dear mother, you will, I know, concede that marriage without love is unholy. I am not able to force myself to love some great lady, even supposing I could win her if I did love her."

"But you might keep yourself from forming a foolish and unworthy attachment," Mrs Stuart interrupted. "With your will-power, your brain, your reasoning faculties, I see no necessity for your allowing a pretty face to run away with your heart. Nothing could be more unsuitable, more shocking, more dreadful, than to have you make that girl your wife, Arthur."

Mrs Stuart's voice rose as she spoke, from a quiet reasoning tone to a high, excited wail. She had not meant to say so much. She had intended merely to appeal to her son's affection for her, without making any unpleasant disclosures regarding Joy's mother; she thought merely to win a promise from him that he would not compromise himself at present with the girl, through an excess of sympathy. But already she had said enough to arouse the young man into a defender of the girl he loved.

"I think your language quite too strong, mother," he said, with a reproving tone in his voice. "Miss Irving is good, gifted, amiable, beautiful, beside being young and full of health. I am sure there could be nothing shocking or dreadful in any man's uniting his destiny with such a being, in case he was fortunate enough to win her. The fact that she is poor, and not of illustrious lineage, is but a very worldly consideration. Mr Irving was a most intelligent and excellent man, even if he was a grocer. The American idea of aristocracy is grotesquely absurd at the best. A man may spend his time and strength in buying and selling things wherewith to clothe the body, and, if he succeeds, his children are admitted to the intimacy of princes; but no success can open that door to the children of a man who trades in food, wherewith to sustain the body. We can none of us afford to put on airs here in America, with butchers and Dutch peasant traders only three or four generations back of our 'best families.' As for me, mother, remember my loved father was a broker. That would damn him in the eyes of some people, you know, cultured gentleman as he was."

Mrs Stuart sat very still, breathing hard and trying to gain control of herself for some moments after her son ceased speaking. He, too, had said more than he intended, and he was sorry that he had hurt his mother's feelings as he saw her evident agitation. But as he rose to go forward and beg her pardon, she spoke.

"The person of whom we were speaking has nothing whatever to do with Mr Irving," she said. "Joy Irving was born before her mother was married. Mrs Irving has a most infamous past, and I would rather see you dead than the husband of her child. You certainly would not want your children to inherit the propensities of such a grandmother? And remember the curse descends to the third and fourth generations. If you doubt my words, go to the Baroness. She knows the whole story, but has revealed it to no one but me."

Mrs Stuart left the room, closing the door behind her as she went. She did not want to be obliged to go over the details of the story which she had heard; she had made her statement, one which she knew must startle and horrify her son, with his high ideals of womanly purity, and she left him to review the situation in silence. It was several hours before the rector left his room.

When he did, he went, not to the Baroness, but directly to Mrs Irving. They were alone for more than an hour. When he emerged from the room, his face was as white as death, and he did not look at Joy as she accompanied him to the door.

Two days later Mrs Irving died.

CHAPTER XV

The congregation of St Blank's Church was rendered sad and solicitous by learning that its rector was on the eve of nervous prostration, and that his physician had ordered a change of air. He went away in company with his mother for a vacation of three months. The day after his departure Joy Irving received a letter from him which read as follows:-

"My Dear Miss Irving,--You may not in your deep grief have given me a thought. If such a thought has been granted one so unworthy, it must have taken the form of surprise that your rector and friend has made no call of condolence since death entered your household. I want to write one little word to you, asking you to be lenient in your judgment of me. I am ill in body and mind. I feel that I am on the eve of some distressing malady. I am not able to reason clearly, or to judge what is right and what is wrong. I am as one tossed between the laws of God and the laws made by men, and bruised in heart and in soul. I dare not see you or speak to you while I am in this state of mind. I fear for what I may say or do. I have not slept since I last saw you. I must go away and gain strength and equilibrium. When I return I shall hope to be master of myself. Until then, adieu. "ARTHUR EMERSON STUART."

These wild and incoherent phrases stirred the young girl's heart with intense pain and anxiety. She had known for almost a year that she loved the young rector; she had believed that he cared for her, and without allowing herself to form any definite thoughts of the future, she had lived in a blissful consciousness of loving and being loved, which is to the fulfilment of a love dream, like inhaling the perfume of a rose, compared to the gathered flower and its attending thorns.

The young clergyman's absence at the time of her greatest need had caused her both wonder and pain. His letter but increased both sentiments without explaining the cause.

It increased, too, her love for him, for whenever over-anxiety is aroused for one dear to us, our love is augmented.

She felt that the young man was in some great trouble, unknown to her, and she longed to be able to comfort him. Into the maiden's tender and ardent affection stole the wifely wish to console and the motherly impulse to protect her dear one from pain, which are strong elements in every real woman's love.

Mrs Irving had died without writing one word to the Baroness; and that personage was in a state of constant excitement until she heard of the rector's plans for rest and travel. Mrs Stuart informed her of the conversation which had taken place between herself and her son; and of his evident distress of mind, which had reacted on his body and made it necessary for him to give up mental work for a season.

"I feel that I owe you a debt of gratitude, dear Baroness," Mrs Stuart had said. "Sad as this condition of things is, imagine how much worse it would be, had my son, through an excess of sympathy for that girl at this time, compromised himself with her before we learned the terrible truth regarding her birth. I feel sure my son will regain his health after a few months' absence, and that he will not jeopardise my happiness and his future by any further thoughts of this unfortunate girl, who in the meantime may not be here when we return."

The Baroness made a mental resolve that the girl should not be there.

While the rector's illness and proposed absence was sufficient evidence that he had resolved upon sacrificing his love for Joy on the altar of duty to his mother and his calling, yet the Baroness felt that danger lurked in the air while Miss Irving occupied her present position. No sooner had Mrs Stuart and her son left the city, than the Baroness sent an anonymous letter to the young organist. It read:

"I do not know whether your mother imparted the secret of her past life to you before she died, but as that secret is known to several people, it seems cruelly unjust that you are kept in ignorance of it. You are not Mr Irving's child. You were born before your mother married. While it is not your fault, only your misfortune, it would be wise for you to go where the facts are not so well known as in the congregation of St Blank's. There are people in that congregation who consider you guilty of a wilful deception in wearing the name you do, and of an affront to good taste in accepting the position you occupy. Many people talk of leaving the church on your account. Your gifts as a musician would win you a position elsewhere, and as I learn that your mother's life was insured for a considerable sum, I am sure you are able to seek new fields where you can bide your disgrace.

"A WELL-WISHER."

Quivering with pain and terror, the young girl cast the letter into the fire, thinking that it was the work of one of those half-crazed beings whose mania takes the form of anonymous letters to unoffending people. Only recently such a person had been brought into the courts for this offence. It occurred to her also that it might be the work of someone who wished to obtain her position as organist of St Blank's. Musicians, she knew, were said to be the most jealous of all people, and while she had never suffered from them before, it might be that her time had now come to experience the misfortunes of her profession.

Tender-hearted and kindly in feeling to all humanity, she felt a sickening sense of sorrow and fear at the thought that there existed such a secret enemy for her anywhere in the world.

She went out upon the street, and for the first time in her life she experienced a sense of suspicion and distrust toward the people she met; for the first time in her life, she realised that the world was not all kind and ready to give her back the honest friendship and the sweet good-will which filled her heart for all her kind. Strive as she would, she could not cast off the depression caused by this vile letter. It was her first experience of this cowardly and despicable phase of human malice, and she felt wounded in soul as by a poisoned arrow shot in the dark. And then, suddenly, there came to her the memory of her mother's words--"If unhappiness ever comes to you, read this letter."

Surely this was the time she needed to read that letter. That it contained some secret of her mother's life she felt sure, and she was equally sure that it contained nothing that would cause her to blush for that beloved mother.

"Whatever the manuscript may have to reveal to me," she said, "it is time that I should know." She took the package from the hiding place, and broke the seal. Slowly she read it to the end, as if anxious to make no error in understanding every phase of the long story it related. Beginning with the marriage of her mother to the French professor, Berene gave a detailed account of her own sad and troubled life, and the shadow which the father's appetite for drugs cast over her whole youth.

"They say," she wrote, "that there is no personal devil in existence. I think this is true; he has taken the form of drugs and spirituous liquors, and so his work of devastation goes on." Then followed the story of the sacrilegious marriage to save her father from suicide, of her early widowhood; and the proffer of the Baroness to give her a home. Of her life of servitude there, her yearning for an education, and her meeting with "Apollo," as she designated Preston Cheney. "For truly he was like the glory of the rising day to me, the first to give me hope, courage and unselfish aid. I loved him, I worshipped him. He loved me, but he strove to crush and kill this love because he had worked out an ambitious career for himself. To extricate himself from many difficulties and embarrassments, and to further his ambitious dreams, he betrothed himself to the daughter of a rich and powerful man. He made no profession of love, and she asked none. She was incapable of giving or inspiring that holy passion. She only asked to be married.

"I only asked to be loved. Knowing nothing of the terrible conflict in his breast, knowing nothing of his new-made ties, I was wounded to the soul by his speaking unkindly to me--words he forced himself to speak to hide his real feelings. And then it was that a strange fate caused him to find me fainting, suffering, and praying for death. The love in both hearts could no longer be restrained. Augmented by its long control, sharpened by the agony we had both suffered, overwhelmed by the surprise of the meeting, we lost reason and prudence. Everything was forgotten save our love. When it was too late I foresaw the anguish and sorrow I must bring into this man's life. I fear it was this thought rather than repentance for sin which troubled me. Well may you ask why I did not think of all this before instead of after the error was committed. Why did not Eve realise the consequences of the fall until she had eaten of the apple? Only afterward did I learn of the unholy ties which my lover had formed that very day--ties which he swore to me should be broken ere another day passed, to render him free to make me his wife in the eyes of men, as I already was in the sight of God.

"Yet a strange and sudden resolve came to me as I listened to him. Far beyond the thought of my own ruin, rose the consciousness of the ruin I should bring upon his life by allowing him to carry out his design. To be his wife, his helpmate, chosen from the whole world as one he deemed most worthy and most able to cheer and aid him in life's battle--that seemed heaven to me; but to know that by one rash, impetuous act of folly, I had placed him in a position where he felt that honour compelled him to marry me--why, this thought was more bitter than death. I knew that he loved me; yet I knew, too, that by a union with me under the circumstances he would antagonise those who were now his best and most influential friends, and that his entire career would be ruined. I resolved to go away; to disappear from his life and leave no trace. If his love was as sincere as mine, he would find me; and time would show him some wiser way for breaking his new-made fetters than the rash and sudden method he now contemplated. He had forgotten to protect me with his love, but I could not forget to protect him. In every true woman's love there is the maternal element which renders sacrifice natural.

"Fate hastened and furthered my plans for departure. Made aware that the Baroness was suspicious of my fault, and learning that my lover was suddenly called to the bedside of his fiancee, I made my escape from the town and left no trace behind. I went to that vast haystack of lost needles--New York, and effaced Berene Dumont in Mrs Lamont. The money left from my father's belongings I resolved to use in cultivating my voice. I advertised for embroidery and fine sewing also, and as I was an expert with the needle, I was able to support myself and lay aside a little sum each week. I trimmed hats at a small price, and added to my income in various manners, owing to my French taste and my deft fingers.

"I was desolate, sad, lonely, but not despairing. What woman can despair when she knows herself loved? To me that consciousness was a far greater source of happiness than would have been the knowledge that I was an empress, or the wife of a millionaire, envied by the whole world. I believed my lover would find me in time, that we should be reunited. I believed this until I saw the announcement of his marriage in the press, and read that he and his bride had sailed for an extended foreign tour; but with this stunning news, there came to me the strange, sweet, startling consciousness that you, my darling child, were coming to console me.

"I know that under the circumstances I ought to have been borne down to the earth with a guilty shame; I ought to have considered you as a punishment for my sin--and walked in the valley of humiliation and despair.

"But I did not. I lived in a state of mental exaltation; every thought was a prayer, every emotion was linked with religious fervour. I was no longer alone or friendless, for I had you. I sang as I had never sung, and one theatrical manager, who happened to call upon my teacher during my lesson hour, offered me a position at a good salary at once if I would accept.

"I could not accept, of course, knowing what the coming months were to bring to me, but I took his card and promised to write him when I was ready to take a position. You came into life in the depressing atmosphere of a city hospital, my dear child, yet even there I was not depressed, and your face wore a smile of joy the first time I gazed upon it. So I named you Joy--and well have you worn the name. My first sorrow was in being obliged to leave you; for I had to leave you with those human angels, the sweet sisters of charity, while I went forth to make a home for you. My voice, as is sometimes the case, was richer, stronger and of greater compass after I had passed through maternity. I accepted a position with a travelling theatrical company, where I was to sing a solo in one act. My success was not phenomenal, but it WAS success nevertheless. I followed this life for three years, seeing you only at intervals. Then the consciousness came to me that without long and profound study I could never achieve more than a third-rate success in my profession.

"I had dreamed of becoming a great singer; but I learned that a voice alone does not make a great singer. I needed years of study, and this would necessitate the expenditure of large sums of money. I had grown heart-sick and disgusted with the annoyances and vulgarity I was subjected to in my position. When you were four years old a good man offered me a good home as his wife. It was the first honest love I had encountered, while scores of men had made a pretence of loving me during these years.

"I was hungering for a home where I could claim you and have the joy of your daily companionship instead of brief glimpses of you at the intervals of months. My voice, never properly trained, was beginning to break. I resolved to put Mr Irving to a test; I would tell him the true story of your birth, and if he still wished me to be his wife, I would marry him.

"I carried out my resolve, and we were married the day after he had heard my story. I lived a peaceful and even happy life with Mr Irving. He was devoted to you, and never by look, word or act, seemed to remember my past. I, too, at times almost forgot it, so strange a thing is the human heart under the influence of time. Imagine, then, the shock of remembrance and the tidal wave of memories which swept over me when in the lady you brought to call upon me I recognised--the

Baroness.

"It is because she threatened to tell you that you were not born in wedlock that I leave this manuscript for you. It is but a few weeks since you told me the story of Marah Adams, and assured me that you thought her mother did right in confessing the truth to her daughter. Little did you dream with what painful interest I listened to your views on that subject. Little did I dream that I should so soon be called upon to act upon them.

"But the time is now come, and I want no strange hand to deal you a blow in the dark; if any part of the story comes to you, I want you to know the whole truth. You will wonder why I have not told you the name of your father. It is strange, but from the hour I knew of his marriage, and of your dawning life, I have felt a jealous fear lest he should ever take you from me; even after I am gone, I would not have him know of your existence and be unable to claim you openly. Any acquaintance between you could only result in sorrow.

"I have never blamed him for my past weakness, however I have blamed him for his unholy marriage. Our fault was mutual. I was no ignorant child; while young in years, I had sufficient knowledge of human nature to protect myself had I used my will-power and my reason. Like many another woman, I used neither; unlike the majority, I did not repent my sin or its consequences. I have ever believed you to be a more divinely born being than any children who may have resulted from my lover's unholy marriage. I die strong in the belief. God bless you, my dear child, and farewell."

Joy sat silent and pale like one in a trance for a long time after she had finished reading. Then she said aloud, "So I am another like Marah Adams; it was this knowledge which caused the rector to write me that strange letter. It was this knowledge which sent him away without coming to say one word of adieu. The woman who sent me the message, sent it to him also. Well, I can be as brave as my mother was. I, too, can disappear."

She arose and began silently and rapidly to make preparations for a journey. She felt a nervous haste to get away from something--from all things. Everything stable in the world seemed to have slipped from her hold in the last few days. Home, mother, love, and now hope and pride were gone too. She worked for more than two hours without giving vent to even a sigh. Then suddenly she buried her face in her hands and sobbed aloud: "Oh, mother, mother, you were not ashamed, but I am ashamed for you! Why was I ever born? God forgive me for the sinful thought, but I wish you had lied to me in place of telling me the truth."

CHAPTER XVI

Just as Mrs Irving had written her story for her daughter to read, she told it, in the main, to the rector a few days before her death.

Only once before had the tale passed her lips; then her listener was Horace Irving; and his only comment was to take her in his arms and place the kiss betrothal on her lips. Never again was the painful subject referred to between them. So imbued had Berene Dumont become with her belief in the legitimacy of her child, and in her own purity, that she felt but little surprise at the calm manner in which Mr Irving received her story, and now when the rector of St Blank's Church was her listener, she expected the same broad judgment to be given her. But it was the calmness of a great and all-forgiving love which actuated Mr Irving, and overcame all other feelings.

Wholly unconventional in nature, caring nothing and knowing little of the extreme ideas of orthodox society on these subjects, the girl Berene and the woman Mrs Irving had lived a life so wholly secluded from the world at large, so absolutely devoid of intimate friendships, so absorbed in her own ideals, that she was incapable of understanding the conventional opinion regarding a woman with a history like hers.

In all those years she had never once felt a sensation of shame. Mr Irving had requested her to rear Joy in the belief that she was his child. As the matter could in no way concern anyone else, Mrs Irving's lips had remained sealed on the subject; but not with any idea of concealing a disgrace. She could not associate disgrace with her love for Preston Cheney. She believed herself to be his spiritual widow, as it were. His mortal clay and legal name only belonged to his wife.

Mr Irving had met Berene on a railroad train, and had conceived one of those sudden and intense passions with which a woman with a past often inspires an innocent and unworldly young man. He was sincerely and truly religious by nature, and as spotless as a maiden in mind and body.

When he had dreamed of a wife, it was always of some shy, innocent girl whom he should woo almost from her mother's arms; some gentle, pious maid, carefully reared, who would help him to establish the Christian household of his imagination. He had thought that love would first come to him as admiring respect, then tender friendship, then love for some such maiden; instead it had swooped down upon him in the form of an intense passion for an absolute stranger--a woman travelling with a theatrical company. He was like a sleeper who awakens suddenly and finds a scorching midday sun beating upon his eyes. A wrecked freight train upon the track detained for several hours the car in which they travelled. The passengers waived ceremony and conversed to pass the time, and Mr Irving learnt Berene's name, occupation and destination. He followed her for a week, and at the end of that time asked her hand in marriage.

Even after he had heard the story of her life, he was not deterred from his resolve to make her his wife. All the Christian charity of his nature, all its chivalry was aroused, and he believed he was plucking a brand from the burning. He never repented his act. He lived wholly for his wife and child, and for the good he could do with them as his faithful allies. He drew more and more away from all the allurements of the world, and strove to rear Joy in what he believed to be a purely Christian life, and to make his wife forget, if possible, that she had ever known a sorrow. All of sincere gratitude, tenderness, and gentle affection possible for her to feel, Berene bestowed upon her husband during his life, and gave to his memory after he was gone.

Joy had been excessively fond of Mr Irving, and it was the dread of causing her a deep sorrow in the knowledge that she was not his child, and the fear that Preston Cheney would in any way interfere with her possession of Joy, which had distressed the mother during the visit of the Baroness, rather than unwillingness to have her sin revealed to her daughter. Added to this, the intrusion of the Baroness into this long hidden and sacred experience seemed a sacrilege from which she shrank with horror. But she now told the tale to Arthur Stuart frankly and fearlessly.

He had asked her to confide to him whatever secret existed regarding Joy's birth.

"There is a rumour afloat," he said, "that Joy is not Mr Irving's child. I love your daughter, Mrs Irving, and I feel it is my right to know all the circumstances of her life. I believe the story which was told my mother to be the invention of some enemy who is jealous of Joy's beauty and talents, and I would like to be in a position to silence these slanders."

So Mrs Irving told the story to the end; and having told it, she felt relieved and happy in the thought that it was imparted to the only two people whom it could concern in the future.

No disturbing fear came to her that the rector would hesitate to make Joy his wife. To Berene Dumont, love was the law. If love existed between two souls she could not understand why any convention of society should stand in the way of its fulfilment.

Arthur Stuart in his role of spiritual confessor and consoler had never before encountered such a phase of human nature. He had listened to many a tale of sin and folly from women's lips, but always had the sinner bemoaned her sin, and bitterly repented her weakness. Here instead was what the world would consider a fallen woman, who on her deathbed regarded her weakness as her strength, her shame as her glory, and who seemed to expect him to take the same view of the matter. When he attempted to urge her to repent, the words stuck in his throat. He left the deathbed of the unfortunate sinner without having expressed one of the conflicting emotions which filled his heart. But he left it with such a weight on his soul, such distress on his mind that death seemed to him the only way of escape from a life of torment.

His love for Joy Irving was not killed by the story he had heard. But it had received a terrible shock, and the thought of making her his wife with the probability that the Baroness would spread the scandal broadcast, and that his marriage would break his mother's heart, tortured him. Added to this were his theories on heredity, and the fear that there might, nay, must be, some dangerous tendency hidden in the daughter of a mother who had so erred, and who in dying showed no comprehension of the enormity of her sin. Had Mrs Irving bewailed her fall, and represented herself as the victim of a wily villain, the rector would not have felt so great a fear of the daughter's inheritance. A frail, repentant woman he could pity and forgive, but it seemed to him that Mrs Irving was utterly lacking in moral nature. She was spiritually blind. The thought tortured him. To leave Joy at this time without calling to see her seemed base and cowardly; yet he dared not trust himself in her presence. So he sent her the strangely worded letter, and went away hoping to be shown the path of duty before he returned.

At the end of three months he came home stronger in body and mind. He had resolved to compromise with fate; to continue his calls upon Joy Irving; to be her friend and rector only, until by the passage of time, and the changes which occur so rapidly in every society, the scandal in regard to her birth had been forgotten. And until by patience and tenderness, he won his mother's consent to the union. He felt that all this must come about as he desired, if he did not aggravate his mother's feeling or defy public opinion by too precipitate methods.

He could not wholly give up all thoughts of Joy Irving. She had grown to be a part of his hopes and dreams of the future, as she was a part of the reality of his present. But she was very young; he could afford to wait, and while he waited to study the girl's character, and if he saw any budding shoot which bespoke the maternal tree, to prune and train it to his own liking. For the sake of his unborn children he felt it his duty to carefully study any woman he thought to make his wife.

But when he reached home, the surprising intelligence awaited him that Miss Irving had left the metropolis. A brief note to the church authorities, resigning her position, and saying that she was about to leave the city, was all that anyone knew of her.

The rector instituted a quiet search, but only succeeded in learning that she had conducted her preparations for departure with the greatest secrecy, and that to no one had she imparted her plans.

Whenever a young woman shrouds her actions in the garments of secrecy, she invites suspicion. The people who love to suspect their fellow-beings of wrong-doing were not absent on this occasion.

The rector was hurt and wounded by all this, and while he resented the intimation from another that Miss Irving's conduct had been peculiar and mysterious, he felt it to be so in his own heart.

"Is it her mother's tendency to adventure developing in her?" he asked himself.

Yet he wrote her a letter, directing it to her at the old number, thinking she would at least leave her address with the post-office for the forwarding of mail. The letter was returned to him from that cemetery of many a dear hope, the dead-letter office. A personal in a leading paper failed to elicit a reply. And then one day six months after the disappearance of Joy Irving, the young rector was called to the Cheney household to offer spiritual consolation to Miss Alice, who believed herself to be dying. She had been in a decline ever since the rector went away for his health.

Since his return she had seen him but seldom, rarely save in the pulpit, and for the last six weeks she had been too ill to attend divine service.

It was Preston Cheney himself, at home upon one of his periodical visits, who sent for the rector, and gravely met him at the door when he arrived, and escorted him into his study.

"I am very anxious about my daughter," he said. "She has been a nervous child always, and over-sensitive. I returned yesterday after an absence of some three months in California, to find Alice in bed, wasted to a shadow, and constantly weeping. I cannot win her confidence--she has never confided to me. Perhaps it is my fault; perhaps I have not been at home enough to make her realise that the relationship of father and daughter is a sacred one. This morning when I was urging her to tell me what grieved her, she remarked that there was but one person to whom she could communicate this sorrow-- her rector. So, my dear Dr Stuart, I have sent for you. I will conduct you to my child, and I leave her in your hands. Whatever comfort and consolation you can offer, I know will be given. I hope she will not bind you to secrecy; I hope you may be able to tell me what troubles her, and advise me how to help her."

It was more than an hour before the rector returned to the library where Preston Cheney awaited him. When the senator heard his approaching step, he looked up, and was startled to see the pallor on the young man's face. "You have something sad, something terrible to tell me!" he cried. "What is it?"

The rector walked across the room several times, breathing deeply, and with anguish written on his countenance. Then he took Senator Cheney's hand and wrung it. "I have an embarrassing announcement to make to you," he said. "It is something so surprising, so unexpected, that I am completely unnerved."

"You alarm me, more and more," the senator answered. "What can be the secret which my frail child has imparted to you that should so distress you? Speak; it is my right to know."

The rector took another turn about the room, and then came and stood facing Senator Cheney.

"Your daughter has conceived a strange passion for me," he said in a low voice. "It is this which has caused her illness, and which she says will cause her death, if I cannot return it."

"And you?" asked his listener after a moment's silence.

"I? Why, I have never thought of your daughter in any such manner," the young man replied. "I have never dreamed of loving her, or winning her love."

"Then do not marry her," Preston Cheney said quietly. "Marriage without love is unholy. Even to save life it is unpardonable."

The rector was silent, and walked the room with nervous steps. "I must go home and think it all out," he said after a time. "Perhaps Miss Cheney will find her grief less, now that she has imparted it to me. I am alarmed at her condition, and I shall hope for an early report from you regarding her."

The report was made twelve hours later. Miss Cheney was delirious, and calling constantly for the rector. Her physician feared the worst.

The rector came, and his presence at once soothed the girl's delirium.

"History repeats itself," said Preston Cheney meditatively to himself. "Alice is drawing this man into the net by her alarming physical condition, as Mabel riveted the chains about me when her mother died.

"But Alice really loves the rector, I think, and she is capable of a much stronger passion than her mother ever felt; and the rector loves no other woman at least, and so this marriage, if it takes place, will not be so wholly wicked and unholy as mine was."

The marriage did take place three months later. Alice Cheney was not the wife whom Mrs Stuart would have chosen for her son, yet she urged him to this step, glad to place a barrier for all time between him and Joy Irving, whose possible return at any day she constantly feared, and whose power over her son's heart she knew was undiminished.

Alice Cheney's family was of the best on both sides; there were wealth, station, and honour; and a step-grandmamma who could be referred to on occasions as "The

Baroness." And there was no skeleton to be hidden or excused.

And Arthur Stuart, believing that Alice Cheney's life and reason depended upon his making her his wife, resolved to end the bitter struggle with his own heart and with fate, and do what seemed to be his duty, toward the girl and toward his mother. When the wedding took place, the saddest face at the ceremony, save that of the groom, was the face of the bride's father. But the bride was radiant, and Mabel and the Baroness walked in clouds.

CHAPTER XVII

Alice did not rally in health or spirits after her marriage, as her family, friends and physician had anticipated. She remained nervous, ailing and despondent.

"Should maternity come to her, she would doubtless be very much improved in health afterward," the doctor said, and Mabel, remembering how true a similar prediction proved in her case, despite her rebellion against it, was not sorry when she knew that Alice was to become a mother, scarcely a year after her marriage.

But Alice grew more and more despondent as the months passed by; and after the birth of her son, the young mother developed dementia of the most hopeless kind. The best specialists in two worlds were employed to bring her out of the state of settled melancholy into which she had fallen, but all to no avail. At the end of two years, her case was pronounced hopeless. Fortunately the child died at the age of six weeks, so the seed of insanity which in the first Mrs Lawrence was simply a case of "nerves," growing into the plant hysteria in Mabel, and yielding the deadly fruit of insanity in Alice, was allowed by a kind providence to become extinct in the fourth generation.

This disaster to his only child caused a complete breaking down of spirit and health in Preston Cheney.

Like some great, strongly coupled car, which loses its grip and goes plunging down an incline to destruction, Preston Cheney's will-power lost its hold on life, and he went down to the valley of death with frightful speed.

During the months which preceded his death, Senator Cheney's only pleasure seemed to be in the companionship of his son-in-law. The strong attachment between the two men ripened with every day's association. One day the rector was sitting by the invalid's couch, reading aloud, when Preston Cheney laid his hand on the young man's arm and said: "Close your book and let me tell you a true story which is stranger than fiction. It is the story of an ambitious man and all the disasters which his realised ambition brought into the lives of others. It is a story whose details are known to but two beings on earth, if indeed the other being still exists on earth. I have long wanted to tell you this story--indeed, I wanted to tell it to you before you made Alice your wife, yet the fear that I would be wrecking the life and reason of my child kept me silent. No doubt if I had told you, and you had been influenced by my experience against a loveless marriage, I should to-day be blaming myself for her condition, which I see plainly now is but the culmination of three generations of hysterical women. But I want to tell you the story and urge you to use it as a warning in your position of counsellor and friend of ambitious young men.

"No matter what else a man may do for position, don't let him marry a woman he does not love, especially if he crucifies a vital passion for another, in order to do this." Then Preston Cheney told the story of his life to his son-in-law; and as the tale proceeded, a strange interest which increased until it became violent excitement, took possession of the rector's brain and heart. The story was so familiar--so very familiar; and at length, when the name of BERENE DUMONT escaped the speaker's lips, Arthur Stuart clutched his hands and clenched his teeth to keep silent until the end of the story came.

"From the hour Berene disappeared, to this very day, no word or message ever came from her," the invalid said. "I have never known whether she was dead or alive, married, or, terrible thought, perhaps driven into a reckless life by her one false step with me. This last fear has been a constant torture to me all these years.

"The world is cruel in its judgment of woman. And yet I know that it is woman herself who has shaped the opinions of the world regarding these matters. If men had had their way since the world began, there would be no virtuous women. Woman has realised this fact, and she has in consequence walled herself about with rules and conventions which have in a measure protected her from man. When any woman breaks through these conventions and errs, she suffers the scorn of others who have kept these self-protecting and society-protecting laws; and, conscious of their scorn, she believes all hope is lost for ever.

"The fear that Berene took this view of her one mistake, and plunged into a desperate life, has embittered my whole existence. Never before did a man suffer such a mental hell as I have endured for this one act of sin and weakness. Yet the world, looking at my life of success, would say if it knew the story, 'Behold how the man goes free.' Free! Great God! there is no bondage so terrible as that of the mind. I have loved Berene Dumont with a changeless passion for twenty-three years, and there has not been a day in all that time that I have not during some hours endured the agonies of the damned, thinking of all the disasters and misery that might have come into her life through me. Heaven knows I would have married her if she had remained. Strange and intricate as the net was which the devil wove about me when I had furnished the cords, I could and would have broken through it after that strange night--at once the heaven and the hell of my memory--if Berene had remained. As it was--I married Mabel, and you know what a farce, ending in a tragedy, our married life has been. God grant that no worse woes befell Berene; God grant that I may meet her in the spirit world and tell her how I loved her and longed for her companionship."

The young rector's eyes were streaming with tears, as he reached over and clasped the sick man's hands in his. "You will meet her," he said with a choked voice. "I heard this same story, but without names, from Berene Dumont's dying lips more than two years ago. And just as Berene disappeared from you--so her daughter disappeared from me; and, God help me, dear father--doubly now my father, I crushed out my great passion for the glorious natural child of your love, to marry the loveless, wretched and UNNATURAL child of your marriage."

The sick man started up on his couch, his eyes flaming, his cheeks glowing with sudden lustre.

"My child--the natural child of Berene's love and mine, you say; oh, my God, speak and tell me what you mean; speak before I die of joy so terrible it is like anguish."

So then it became the rector's turn to take the part of narrator. When the story was ended, Preston Cheney lay weeping like a woman on his couch; the first tears he had shed since his mother died and left him an orphan of ten.

"Berene living and dying almost within reach of my arms--almost within sound of my voice!" he cried. "Oh, why did I not find her before the grave closed between us?--and why did no voice speak from that grave to tell me when I held my daughter's hand in mine?--my beautiful child, no wonder my heart went out to her with such a gush of tenderness; no wonder I was fired with unaccountable anger and indignation when Mabel and Alice spoke unkindly of her. Do you remember how her music stirred me? It was her mother's heart speaking to mine through the genius of our child.

"Arthur, you must find her--you must find her for me! If it takes my whole fortune I must see my daughter, and clasp her in my arms before I die."

But this happiness was not to be granted to the dying man. Overcome by the excitement of this new emotion, he grew weaker and weaker as the next few days passed, and at the end of the fifth day his spirit took its flight, let us hope to join its true mate.

It had been one of his dying requests to have his body taken to Beryngford and placed beside that of Judge Lawrence.

The funeral services took place in the new and imposing church edifice which had been constructed recently in Beryngford. The quiet interior village had taken a leap forward during the last few years, and was now a thriving city, owing to the discovery of valuable stone quarries in its borders.

The Baroness and Mabel had never been in Beryngford since the death of Judge Lawrence many years before; and it was with sad and bitter hearts that both women recalled the past and realised anew the disasters which had wrecked their dearest hopes and ambitions.

The Baroness, broken in spirit and crushed by the insanity of her beloved Alice, now saw the form of the man whom she had hopelessly loved for so many years, laid away to crumble back to dust; and yet, the sorrows which should have softened her soul, and made her heart tender toward all suffering humanity, rendered her pitiless as the grave toward one lonely and desolate being before the shadows of night had fallen upon the grave of Preston Cheney.

When the funeral march pealed out from the grand new organ during the ceremonies in the church, both the Baroness and the rector, absorbed as they were in mournful sorrow, started with surprise. Both gazed at the organ loft; and there, before the great instrument, sat the graceful figure of Joy Irving. The rector's face grew pale as the corpse in the casket; the withered cheek of the Baroness turned a sickly yellow, and a spark of anger dried the moisture in her eyes.

Before the night had settled over the thriving city of Beryngford, the Baroness dropped a point of virus from the lancet of her tongue to poison the social atmosphere where Joy Irving had by the merest accident of fate made her new home, and where in the office of organist she had, without dreaming of her dramatic situation, played the requiem at the funeral of her own father.

CHAPTER XVIII

J oy Irving had come to Beryngford at the time when the discoveries of the quarries caused that village to spring into sudden prominence as a growing city. Newspaper accounts of the building of the new church, and the purchase of a large pipe organ, chanced to fall under her eye just as she was planning to leave the scene of her unhappiness.

"I can at least only fail if I try for the position of organist there," she said, "and if I succeed in this interior town, I can hide myself from all the world without incurring heavy expense."

So all unconsciously Joy fled from the metropolis to the very place from which her mother had vanished twenty-two years before.

She had been the organist in the grand new Episcopalian Church now for three years; and she had made many cordial acquaintances who would have become near friends, if she had encouraged them. But Joy's sweet and trustful nature had received a great shock in the knowledge of the shadow which hung about her birth. Where formerly she had expected love and appreciation from everyone she met, she now shrank from forming new ties, lest new hurts should await her.

She was like a flower in whose perfect heart a worm had coiled. Her entire feeling about life had undergone a change. For many weeks after her self-imposed exile, she had been unable to think of her mother without a mingled sense of shame and resentment; the adoring love she had borne this being seemed to die with her respect. After a time the bitterness of this sentiment wore away, and a pitying tenderness and sorrow took its place; but from her heart the twin angels, Love and Forgiveness, were absent. She read her mother's manuscript over, and tried to argue herself into the philosophy which had sustained the author of her being through all these years.

But her mind was shaped far more after the conventional pattern of her paternal ancestors, who had been New England Puritans, and she could not view the subject as Berene had viewed it.

In spite of the ideality which her mother had woven about him, Joy entertained the most bitter contempt for the unknown man who was her father, and the whole tide of her affections turned lavishly upon the memory of Mr Irving, whom she felt now more than ever so worthy of her regard.

Reason as she would on the supremacy of love over law, yet the bold, unpleasant fact remained that she was the child of an unwedded mother. She shrank in sensitive pain from having this story follow her, and the very consciousness that her mother's experience had been an exceptional one, caused her the greater dread of having it known and talked of as a common vulgar liaison.

There are two things regarding which the world at large never asks any questions--namely, How a rich man made his money, and how an erring woman came to fall. It is enough for the world to know that he is rich--that fact alone opens all doors to him, as the fact that the woman has erred closes them to her.

There was a common vulgar creature in Beryngford, whose many amours and bold defiance of law and order rendered her name a synonym for indecency. This woman had begun her career in early girlhood as a mercenary intriguer; and yet Joy Irving knew that the majority of people would make small distinctions between the conduct of this creature and that of her mother, were the facts of Berene's life and her own birth to be made public.

The fear that the story would follow her wherever she went became an absolute dread with her, and caused her to live alone and without companions, in the midst of people who would gladly have become her warm friends, had she permitted.

Her book of "Impressions" reflected the changes which had taken place in the complexion of her mind during these years. Among its entries were the following:-

People talk about following a divine law of love, when they wish to excuse their brute impulses and break social and civil codes.

No love is sanctioned by God, which shatters human hearts.

Fathers are only distantly related to their children; love for the male parent is a matter of education.

The devil macadamises all his pavements.

A natural child has no place in an unnatural world.

When we cannot respect our parents, it is difficult to keep our ideal of God.

Love is a mushroom, and lust is its poisonous counterpart.

It is a pity that people who despise civilisation should be so uncivil as to stay in it. There is always darkest Africa.

The extent of a man's gallantry depends on the goal. He follows the good woman to the borders of Paradise and leaves her with a polite bow; but he follows the bad woman to the depths of hell.

It is easy to trust in God until he permits us to suffer. The dentist seems a skilled benefactor to mankind when we look at his sign from the street. When we sit in his chair he seems a brute, armed with devil's implements.

An anonymous letter is the bastard of a diseased mind.

An envious woman is a spark from Purgatory.

The consciousness that we have anything to hide from the world stretches a veil between our souls and heaven. We cannot reach up to meet the gaze of God, when we are afraid to meet the eyes of men.

It may be all very well for two people to make their own laws, but they have no right to force a third to live by them.

Virtue is very secretive about her payments, but the whole world hears of it when vice settles up.

We have a sublime contempt for public opinion theoretically so long as it favours us. When it turns against us we suffer intensely from the loss of what we claimed to despise.

When the fruit must apologise for the tree, we do not care to save the seed.

It is only when God and man have formed a syndicate and agreed upon their laws, that marriage is a safe investment.

The love that does not protect its object would better change its name.

When we say OF people what we would not say TO them, we are either liars or cowards.

The enmity of some people is the greatest compliment they can pay us.

It was in thoughts like these that Joy relieved her heart of some of the bitterness and sorrow which weighed upon it. And day after day she bore about with her the dread of having the story of her mother's sin known in her new home.

As our fears, like our wishes, when strong and unremitting, prove to be magnets, the result of Joy's despondent fears came in the scandal which the Baroness had planted and left to flourish and grow in Beryngford after her departure. An hour before the services began, on the day of Preston Cheney's burial, Joy learned at whose rites she was to officiate as organist. A pang of mingled emotions shot through her heart at the sound of his name. She had seen this man but a few times, and spoken with him but once; yet he had left a strong impression upon her memory. She had felt drawn to him by his sympathetic face and atmosphere, the sorrow of his kind eyes, and the keen appreciation he had shown in her art; and just in the measure that she had been attracted by him, she had been repelled by the three women to whom she was presented at the same time. She saw them all again mentally, as she had seen them on that and many other days. Mrs Cheney and Alice, with their fretful, plain, dissatisfied faces, and their over-burdened costumes, and the Baroness, with her cruel heart gazing through her worn mask of defaced beauty.

She had been conscious of a feeling of overwhelming pity for the kind, attractive man who made the fourth of that quartette. She knew that he had obtained honours and riches from life, but she pitied him for his home environment. She had felt so thankful for her own happy home life at the time; and she remembered, too, the sweet hope that lay like a closed-up bud in the bottom of her heart that day, as the quartette moved away and left her standing alone with Arthur Stuart.

It was only a few weeks later that the end came to all her dreams, through that terrible anonymous letter.

It was the Baroness who had sent it, she knew--the Baroness whose early hatred for her mother had descended to the child. "And now I must sit in the same house with her again," she said, "and perhaps meet her face to face; and she may tell the story here of my mother's shame, even as I have felt and feared it must yet be told. How strange that a 'love child' should inspire so much hatred!"

Joy had carefully refrained from reading New York papers ever since she left the city; and she had no correspondents. It was her wish and desire to utterly sink and forget the past life there. Therefore she knew nothing of Arthur Stuart's marriage to the daughter of Preston Cheney. She thought of the rector as dead to her.

She believed he had given her up because of the stain upon her birth, and, bitter as the pain had been, she never blamed him. She had fought with her love for him and believed that it was buried in the grave of all other happy memories.

But as the earth is wrenched open by volcanic eruptions and long buried corpses are revealed again to the light of day, so the unexpected sight of Arthur Stuart, as he took his place beside Mabel and the Baroness during the funeral services, revealed all the pent- up passion of her heart to her own frightened soul.

To strong natures, the greater the inward excitement the more quiet the exterior; and Jay passed through the services, and performed her duties, without betraying to those about her the violent emotions under which she laboured.

The rector of Beryngford Church requested her to remain for a few moments, and consult with him on a matter concerning the next week's musical services. It was from him Joy learned the relation which Arthur Stuart bore to the dead man, and that Beryngford was the former home of the Baroness.

Her mother's manuscript had carefully avoided all mention of names of people or places. Yet Joy realised now that she must be living in the very scene of her mother's early life; she longed to make inquiries, but was prevented by the fear that she might hear her mother's name mentioned disrespectfully.

The days that followed were full of sharp agony for her. It was not until long afterward that she was able to write her "impressions" of that experience. In the extreme hour of joy or agony we formulate no impressions; we only feel. We neither analyse nor describe our friends or enemies when face to face with them, but after we leave their presence. When the day came that she could write, some of her reflections were thus epitomised:

Love which rises from the grave to comfort us, possesses more of the demons' than the angels' power. It terrifies us with its supernatural qualities and deprives us temporarily of our reason.

Suppressed steam and suppressed emotion are dangerous things to deal with.

The infant who wants its mother's breast, and the woman who wants her lover's arms, are poor subjects to reason with. Though you tell the former that fever has poisoned the mother's milk, or the latter that destruction lies in the lover's embrace, one heeds you no more than the other.

The accumulated knowledge of ages is sometimes revealed by a kiss. Where wisdom is bliss, it is folly to be ignorant.

Some of us have to crucify our hearts before we find our souls.

A woman cannot fully know charity until she has met passion; but too intimate an acquaintance with the latter destroys her appreciation of all the virtues.

To feel temptation and resist it, renders us liberal in our judgment of all our kind. To yield to it, fills us with suspicion of all.

There is an ecstatic note in pain which is never reached in happiness.

The death of a great passion is a terrible thing, unless the dawn of a greater truth shines on the grave.

Love ought to have no past tense.

Love partakes of the feline nature. It has nine lives.

It seems to be difficult for some of us to distinguish between looseness of views, and charitable judgments. To be sorry for people's sins and follies and to refuse harsh criticism is right; to accept them as a matter of course is wrong.

Love and sorrow are twins, and knowledge is their nurse.

The pathway of the soul is not a steady ascent, but hilly and broken. We must sometimes go lower, in order to get higher.

That which is to-day, and will be to-morrow, must have been yesterday. I know that I live, I believe that I shall live again, and have lived before.

Earth life is the middle rung of a long ladder which we climb in the dark. Though we cannot see the steps below, or above, they exist all the same.

The materialist denying spirit is like the burr of the chestnut denying the meat within.

The inevitable is always right.

Prayer is a skeleton key that opens unexpected doors. We may not find the things we came to seek, but we find other treasures.

The pessimist belongs to God's misfit counter.

Art, when divorced from Religion, always becomes a wanton.

To forget benefits we have received is a crime. To remember benefits we have bestowed is a greater one.

To some men a woman is a valuable book, carefully studied and choicely guarded behind glass doors. To others, she is a daily paper, idly scanned and tossed aside.

CHAPTER XIX

While Joy battled with her sorrow during the days following Preston Cheney's burial, she woke to the consciousness that her history was known in Beryngford. The indescribable change in the manner of her acquaintances, the curiosity in the eyes of some, the insolence or familiarity of others, all told her that her fears were realised; and then there came a letter from the church authorities requesting her to resign her position as organist.

This letter came to the young girl on one of those dreary autumn nights when all the desolation of the dying summer, and none of the exhilaration of the approaching winter, is in the air. She had been labouring all day under a cloud of depression which hovered over her heart and brain and threatened to wholly envelop her; and the letter from the church committee cut her heart like a poniard stroke. Sometimes we are able to bear a series of great disasters with courage and equanimity, while we utterly collapse under some slight misfortune. Joy had been a heroine in her great sorrows, but now in the undeserved loss of her position as church organist, she felt herself unable longer to cope with Fate.

"There's no place for me anywhere," she said to herself. Had she known the truth, that the Baroness had represented her to the committee as a fallen woman of the metropolis, who had left the city for the city's good, the letter would not have seemed to her so cruelly unjust and unjustifiable.

Bitter as had been her suffering at the loss of Arthur Stuart from her life, she had found it possible to understand his hesitation to make her his wife. With his fine sense of family pride, and his reverence for the estate of matrimony, his belief in heredity, it seemed quite natural to her that he should be shocked at the knowledge of the conditions under which she was born; and the thought that her disappearance from his life was helping him to solve a painful problem, had at times, before this unexpected sight of him, rendered her almost happy in her lonely exile. She had grown strangely fond of Beryngford--of the old streets and homes which she knew must have been familiar to her mother's eyes, of the new church whose glorious voiced organ gave her so many hours of comfort and relief of soul, of the tiny apartment where she and her heart communed together. She was catlike in her love of places, and now she must tear herself away from all these surroundings and seek some new spot wherein to hide herself and her sorrows.

It was like tearing up a half-rooted flower, already drooping from one transplanting. She said to herself that she could never survive another change. She read the letter over which lay in her hand, and tears began to slowly well from her eyes. Joy seldom wept; but now it seemed to her she was some other person, who stood apart and wept tears of sympathy for this poor girl, Joy Irving, whose life was so hemmed about with troubles, none of which were of her own making; and then, like a dam which suddenly gives way and allows a river to overflow, a great storm of sobs shook her frame, and she wept as she had never wept before; and with her tears there came rushing back to her heart all the old love and sorrow for the dead mother which had so long been hidden under her burden of shame; and all the old passion and longing for the man whose insane wife she knew to be a more hopeless obstacle between them than this mother's history had proven.

"Mother, Arthur, pity me, pity me!" she cried. "I am all alone, and the strife is so terrible. I have never meant to harm any living thing! Mother Arthur, GOD, how can you all desert me so?"

At last, exhausted, she fell into a deep and dreamless sleep.

She awoke the following morning with an aching head, and a heart wherein all emotions seemed dead save a dull despair. She was conscious of only one wish, one desire--a longing to sit again in the organ loft, and pour forth her soul in one last farewell to that instrument which had grown to seem her friend, confidant and lover.

She battled with her impulse as unreasonable and unwise, till the day was well advanced. But it grew stronger with each hour; and at last she set forth under a leaden sky and through a dreary November rain to the church.

Her head throbbed with pain, and her hands were hot and feverish, as she seated herself before the organ and began to play. But with the first sounds responding to her touch, she ceased to think of bodily discomfort.

The music was the voice of her own soul, uttering to God all its desolation, its anguish and its despair. Then suddenly, with no seeming volition of her own, it changed to a passion of human love, human desire; the sorrow of separation, the strife with the emotions, the agony of renunciation were all there; and the November rain, beating in wild gusts against the window-panes behind the musician, lent a fitting accompaniment to the strains.

She had been playing for perhaps an hour, when a sudden exhaustion seized upon her, and her hands fell nerveless and inert upon her lap; she dropped her chin upon her breast and closed her eyes. She was drunken with her own music.

When she opened them again a few moments later, they fell upon the face of Arthur Stuart, who stood a few feet distant regarding her with haggard eyes. Unexpected and strange as his presence was, Joy felt neither surprise nor wonder. She had been thinking of him so intensely, he had been so interwoven with the music she had been playing, that his bodily presence appeared to her as a natural result. He was the first to speak; and when he spoke she noticed that his voice sounded hoarse and broken, and that his face was drawn and pale.

"I came to Beryngford this morning expressly to see you, Joy," he said. "I have many things to say to you. I went to your residence and was told by the maid that I would find you here. I followed, as you see. We have had many meetings in church edifices, in organ lofts. It seems natural to find you in such a place, but I fear it will be unnatural and unfitting to say to you here, what I came to say. Shall we return to your home?"

His eyes shone strangely from dusky caverns, and there were deep lines about his mouth.

"He, too, has suffered," thought Joy; "I have not borne it all alone." Then she said aloud:

"We are quite undisturbed here; I know of nothing I could listen to in my room which I could not hear you say in this place. Go on."

He looked at her silently for a moment, his cheeks pale, his breast heaving. Before he came to Beryngford, he had fought his battle between religion and human passion, and passion had won. He had cast under his feet every principle and tradition in which he had been reared, and resolved to live alone henceforth for the love and companionship of one human being, could he obtain her consent to go with him.

Yet for the moment, he hesitated to speak the words he had resolved to utter, under the roof of a house of God, so strong were the influences of his early training and his habits of thought. But as his eyes feasted upon the face before him, his hesitation vanished, and he leaned toward her and spoke. "Joy," he said, "three years ago I went away and left you in sorrow, alone, because I was afraid to brave public opinion, afraid to displease my mother and ask you to be my wife. The story your mother told me of your birth, a story she left in manuscript for you to read, made a social coward of me. I was afraid to take a girl born out of wedlock to be my life companion, the mother of my children. Well, I married a girl born in wedlock; and where is my companion?" He paused and laughed recklessly. Then he went on hurriedly: "She is in an asylum for the insane. I am chained to a corpse for life. I had not enough moral courage three-years ago to make you my wife. But I have moral courage enough now to come here and ask you to go with me to Australia, and begin a new life together. My mother died a year ago. I donned the surplice at her bidding. I will abandon it at the bidding of Love. I sinned against heaven in marrying a woman I did not love. I am willing to sin against the laws of man by living with the woman I do love; will you go with me, Joy?" There was silence save for the beating of the rain against the stained window, and the wailing of the wind.

Joy was in a peculiarly overwrought condition of mind and body. Her hours of extravagant weeping the previous night, followed by a day of fasting, left her nervous system in a state to be easily excited by the music she had been playing. She was virtually intoxicated with sorrow and harmony. She was incapable of reasoning, and conscious only of two things--that she must leave Beryngford, and that the man whom she had loved with her whole heart for five years, was asking her to go with him; to be no more homeless, unloved, and alone, but his companion while life should last.

"Answer me, Joy," he was pleading. "Answer me."

She moved toward the stairway that led down to the street door; and as she flitted by him, she said, looking him full in the eyes with a slow, grave smile, "Yes, Arthur, I will go with you."

He sprang toward her with a wild cry of joy, but she was already flying down the stairs and out upon the street.

When he joined her, they walked in silence through the rain to her door, neither speaking a word, until he would have followed her within. Then she laid her hand upon his shoulder and said gently but firmly: "Not now, Arthur; we must not see each other again until we go away. Write me where to meet you, and I will join you within twenty-four hours. Do not urge me--you must obey me this once-- afterward I will obey you. Good-night."

As she closed the door upon him, he said, "Oh, Joy, I have so much to tell you. I promised your father when he was dying that I would find you; I swore to myself that when I found you I would never leave you, save at your own command. I go now, only because you bid me go. When we meet again, there must be no more parting; and you shall hear a story stranger than the wildest fiction--the story of your father's life. Despite your mother's secretiveness regarding this portion of her history, the knowledge has come to me in the most unexpected manner, from the lips of the man himself."

Joy listened dreamily to the words he was saying. Her father--she was to know who her father was? Well, it did not matter much to her now--father, mother, what were they, what was anything save the fact that he had come back to her and that he loved her?

She smiled silently into his eyes. Glance became entangled with glance, and would not be separated.

He pushed open the almost closed door and she felt herself enveloped with arms and lips.

A second later she stood alone, leaning dizzily against the door; heart, brain and blood in a mad riot of emotion.

Then she fell into a chair and covered her burning face with her hands as she whispered, "Mother, mother, forgive me--I understand--I understand."

CHAPTER XX

The first shock of the awakened emotions brings recklessness to some women, and to others fear.

The more frivolous plunge forward like the drunken man who leaps from the open window believing space is water.

The more intense draw back, startled at the unknown world before them.

The woman who thinks love is all ideality is more liable to follow into undreamed-of chasms than she who, through the complexity of her own emotions, realises its grosser elements.

It was long after midnight when Joy fell into a heavy sleep, the night of Arthur Stuart's visit. She heard the drip of the dreary November rain upon the roof, and all the light and warmth seemed stricken from the universe save the fierce fire in her own heart.

When she woke in the late morning, great splashes of sunlight were leaping and quivering like living things across the foot of her bed; she sprang up, dazed for a moment by the flood of light in the room, and went to the window and looked out upon a sun-kissed world smiling in the arms of a perfect Indian summer day.

A happy little sparrow chirped upon the window sill, and some children ran across the street bare-headed, exulting in the soft air. All was innocence and sweetness. Mind and morals are greatly influenced by weather. Many things seem right in the fog and gloom, which we know to be wrong in the clear light of a sunny morning. The events of the previous day came back to Joy's mind as she stood by the window, and stirred her with a sense of strangeness and terror. The thought of the step she had resolved to take brought a sudden trembling to her limbs. It seemed to her the eyes of God were piercing into her heart, and she was afraid.

Joy had from her early girlhood been an earnest and sincere follower of the

Christian religion. The embodiment of love and sympathy herself, it was natural for her to believe in the God of Love and to worship Him in outward forms, as well as in her secret soul. It was the deep and earnest fervour of religion in her heart, which rendered her music so unusual and so inspiring. There never was, is not and never can be greatness in any art where religious feeling is lacking.

There must be the consciousness of the Infinite, in the mind which produces infinite results.

Though the artist be gifted beyond all other men, though he toil unremittingly, so long as he says, "Behold what I, the gifted and tireless toiler, can achieve," he shall produce but mediocre and ephemeral results. It is when he says reverently, "Behold what powers greater than I shall achieve through me, the instrument," that he becomes great and men marvel at his power.

Joy's religious nature found expression in her music, and so something more than a harmony of beautiful sounds impressed her hearers.

The first severe blow to her faith in the church as a divine institution, was when her rector and her lover left her alone in the hour of her darkest trials, because he knew the story of her mother's life. His hesitancy to make her his wife she understood, but his absolute desertion of her at such a time, seemed inconsistent with his calling as a disciple of the Christ.

The second blow came in her dismissal from the position of organist at the Beryngford Church, after the presence of the Baroness in the town.

A disgust for human laws, and a bitter resentment towards society took possession of her. When a gentle and loving nature is roused to anger and indignation, it is often capable of extremes of action; and Arthur Stuart had made his proposition of flight to Joy Irving in an hour when her high-wrought emotions and intensely strung nerves made any desperate act possible to her. The sight of his face, with its evidences of severe suffering, awoke all her smouldering passion for the man; and the thought that he was ready to tread his creed under his feet and to defy society for her sake, stirred her with a wild joy. God had seemed very far away, and human love was very precious; too precious to be thrown away in obedience to any man-made law.

But somehow this morning God seemed nearer, and the consciousness of what she had promised to do terrified her. Disturbed by her thoughts, she turned towards her toilet-table and caught sight of the letter of dismissal from the church committee. It acted upon her like an electric shock. Resentment and indignation re-enthroned themselves in her bosom.

"Is it to cater to the opinions and prejudices of people like THESE that I hesitate to take the happiness offered me?" she cried, as she tore the letter in bits and cast it beneath her feet. Arthur Stuart appeared to her once more, in the light of a delivering angel. Yes, she would go with him to the ends of the earth. It was her inheritance to lead a lawless life. Nothing else was possible for her. God must see how she had been hemmed in by circumstances, how she had been goaded and driven from the paths of peace and purity where she had wished to dwell. God was not a man, and He would be merciful in judging her.

She sent her landlady two months' rent in advance, and notice of her departure, and set hurriedly about her preparations.

Twenty-five years before, when Berene Dumont disappeared from Beryngford, she had, quite unknown to herself, left one devoted though humble friend behind, who sincerely mourned her absence.

Mrs Connor liked to be spoken of as "the wash-lady at the Palace." Yet proud as she was of this appellation, she was not satisfied with being an excellent laundress. She was a person of ambitions. To be the owner of a lodging-house, like the Baroness, was her leading ambition, and to possess a "peany" for her young daughter Kathleen was another.

She kept her mind fixed on these two achievements, and she worked always for those two results. And as mind rules matter, so the laundress became in time the landlady of a comfortable and respectable lodging-house, and in its parlour a piano was the chief object of furniture.

Kathleen Connor learned to play; and at last to the joy of the lodgers, she married and bore her "peany" away with her. During the time when Mrs Connor was the ambitious "wash-lady" at the Palace, Berene Dumont came to live there; and every morning when the young woman carried the tray down to the kitchen after having served the Baroness with her breakfast, she offered Mrs Connor a cup of coffee and a slice of toast.

This simple act of thoughtfulness from the young dependant touched the Irish-woman's tender heart and awoke her lasting gratitude. She had heard Berene's story, and she had been prepared to mete out to her that disdainful dislike which Erin almost invariably feels towards France. Realising that the young widow was by birth and breeding above the station of housemaid, Mrs Connor and the servants had expected her to treat them with the same lofty airs which the Baroness made familiar to her servants. When, instead, Berene toasted the bread for Mrs Connor, and poured the coffee and placed it on the kitchen table with her own hands, the heart of the wash-lady melted in her ample breast. When the heart of the daughter of Erin melts, it permeates her whole being; and Mrs Connor became a secret devotee at the shrine of Miss Dumont.

She had never entertained cordial feelings toward the Baroness. When a society lady--especially a titled one--enters into competition with working people, and yet refuses to associate with them, it always incites their enmity. The working population of Beryngford, from the highest to the lowest grades, felt a sense of resentment toward the Baroness, who in her capacity of landlady still maintained the airs of a grand dame, and succeeded in keeping her footing with some of the most fashionable people in the town.

Added to these causes of dislike, the Baroness was, like many wealthier people, excessively close in her dealings with working folk, haggling over a few cents or a few moments of wasted time, while she was generosity itself in association with her equals.

Mrs Connor, therefore, felt both pity and sympathy for Miss Dumont, whose position in the Palace she knew to be a difficult one; and when Preston Cheney came upon the scene the romantic mind of the motherly Irishwoman fashioned a future for the young couple which would have done credit to the pen of a Mrs Southworth.

Mr Cheney always had a kind word for the laundress, and a tip as well; and when Mrs Connor's dream of seeing him act the part of the Prince and Berene the Cinderella of a modern fairy story, ended in the disappearance of Miss Dumont and the marriage of Mr Cheney to Mabel Lawrence, the unhappy wash-lady mourned unceasingly.

Ten years of hard, unremitting toil and rigid economy passed away before Mrs Connor could realise her ambition of becoming a landlady in the purchase of a small house which contained but four rooms, three of which were rented to lodgers. The increase in the value of her property during the next five years, left the fortunate speculator with a fine profit when she sold her house at the end of that time, and rented a larger one; and as she was an excellent financier, it was not strange that, at the time Joy Irving appeared on the scene, "Mrs Connor's apartments" were as well and favourably known in Beryngford, if not as distinctly fashionable, as the Palace had been more than twenty years ago.

So it was under the roof of her mother's devoted and faithful mourner that the unhappy young orphan had found a home when she came to hide herself away from all who had ever known her.

The landlady experienced the same haunting sensation of something past and gone when she looked on the girl's beautiful face, which had so puzzled the Baroness; a something which drew and attracted the warm heart of the Irishwoman, as the magnet draws the steel. Time and experience had taught Mrs Connor to be discreet in her treatment of her tenants; to curb her curiosity and control her inclination to sociability. But in the case of Miss Irving she had found it impossible to refrain from sundry kindly acts which were not included in the terms of the contract. Certain savoury dishes found their way mysteriously to Miss Irving's menage, and flowers appeared in her room as if by magic, and in various other ways the good heart and intentions of Mrs Connor were unobtrusively expressed toward her favourite tenant. Joy had taken a suite of four rooms, where, with her maid, she lived in modest comfort and complete retirement from the social world of Beryngford, save as the close connection of the church with Beryngford society rendered her, in the position of organist, a participant in many of the social features of the town. While Joy was in the midst of her preparations for departure, Mrs Connor made her appearance with swollen eyes and red, blistered face.

"And it's the talk of that ould witch of a Baroness, may the divil run away with her, that is drivin' ye away, is it?" she cried excitedly; "and it's not Mrs Connor as will consist to the daughter of your mother, God rest her soul, lavin' my house like this. To think that I should have had ye here all these years, and never known ye to be her child till now, and now to see ye driven away by the divil's own! But if it's the fear of not being able to pay the rint because ye've lost your position, ye needn't lave for many a long day to come. It's Mrs Connor would only be as happy as the queen herself to work her hands to the bone for ye, remembering your darlint of a mother, and not belavin' one word against her, nor ye."

So soon as Joy could gain possession of her surprised senses, she calmed the weeping woman and began to question her.

"My good woman," she said, "what are you talking about? Did you ever know my mother, and where did you know her?"

"In the Palace, to be sure, as they called the house of that imp of Satan, the Baroness. I was the wash-lady there, for it's not Mrs Conner the landlady as is above spakin' of the days when she wasn't as high in the world as she is now; and many is the cheerin' cup of coffee or tay from your own mother's hand, that I've had in the forenoon, to chirk me up and put me through my washing, bless her sweet face; and niver have I forgotten her; and niver have I ceased to miss her and the fine young man that took such an interest in her and that I'm as sure loved her, in spite of his marrying the Judge's spook of a daughter, as I am that the Holy Virgin loves us all; and it's a foine man that your father must have been, but young Mr Cheney was foiner."

So little by little Joy drew the story from Mrs Connor and learned the name of the mysterious father, so carefully guarded from her in Mrs Irving's manuscript, the father at whose funeral services she had so recently officiated as organist.

And strangest and most startling of all, she learned that Arthur Stuart's insane wife was her half-sister.

Added to all this, Joy was made aware of the nature of the reports which the Baroness had been circulating about her; and her feeling of bitter resentment and anger toward the church committee was modified by the knowledge that it was not owing to the shadow on her birth, but to the false report of her own evil life, that she had been asked to resign.

After Mrs Connor had gone, Joy was for a long time in meditation, and then turned in a mechanical manner to her delayed task. Her book of "Impressions" lay on a table close at hand.

And as she took it up the leaves opened to the sentence she had written three years before, after her talk with the rector about Marah Adams.

"It seems to me I could not love a man who did not seek to lead me higher; the moment he stood below me and asked me to descend, I should realise he was to be pitied, not adored!"

She shut the book and fell on her knees in prayer; and as she prayed a strange thing happened. The room filled with a peculiar mist, like the smoke which is illuminated by the brilliant rays of the morning sun; and in the midst of it a small square of intense rose-coloured light was visible. This square grew larger and larger, until it assumed the size and form of a man, whose face shone with immortal glory. He smiled and laid his hand on Joy's head. "Child, awake," he said, and with these words vast worlds dawned upon the girl's sight. She stood above and apart from her grosser body, untrammelled and free; she saw long vistas of lives in the past through which she had come to the present; she saw long vistas of lives in the future through which she must pass to gain the experience which would lead her back to God. An ineffable peace and serenity enveloped her. The divine Presence seemed to irradiate the place in which she stood--she felt herself illuminated, transfigured, sanctified by the holy flame within her.

When she came back to the kneeling form by the couch, and rose to her feet, all the aspect of life had changed for her.

CHAPTER XXI

Joy Irving had unpacked her trunks and set her small apartment to rights, when the postman's ring sounded, and a moment later a letter was slipped under her door.

She picked it up, and recognised Arthur Stuart's penmanship. She sat down, holding the unopened letter in her hands.

"It is Arthur's message, appointing a time and place for our meeting," she said to herself. "How long ago that strange interview with him seems!--yet it was only yesterday. How utterly the whole of life has changed for me since then! The universe seems larger, God nearer, and life grander. I am as one who slept and dreamed of darkness and sorrow, and awakes to light and joy."

But when she opened the envelope and read the few hastily written lines within, an exclamation of surprise escaped her lips. It was a brief note from Arthur Stuart and began abruptly without an address (a manner more suggestive of strong passion than any endearing words).

"The first item which my eye fell upon in the telegraphic column of the morning paper, was the death of my wife in the Retreat for the Insane. I leave by the first express to bring her body here for burial.

"A merciful providence has saved us the necessity of defying the laws of God or man, and opened the way for me to claim you before all the world as my worshipped wife so soon as propriety will permit.

"I shall see you at any hour you may indicate after to-morrow, for a brief interview.

"ARTHUR EMERSON STUART."

Joy held the letter in her hand a long time, lost in profound reflection. Then she sat down to her desk and wrote three letters; one was to Mrs Lawrence; one to the chairman of the church committee, who had requested her resignation; the third was to Mr Stuart, and read thus:

"My Dear Mr Stuart,--Many strange things have occurred to me since I saw you. I have learned the name of my father, and this knowledge reveals the fact to me that your unfortunate wife was my half-sister. I have learned, too, that the loss of my position here as organist is not due to the narrow prejudice of the committee regarding the shadow on my birth, but to malicious stories put in circulation by Mrs Lawrence, relating to me.

"Infamous and libellous tales regarding my life have been told, and must be refuted. I have written to Mrs Lawrence demanding a letter from her, clearing my personal character, or giving her the alternative of appearing in court to answer the charge of defamation of character. I have also written to the church committee requesting them to meet me here in my apartments to-morrow, and explain their demand for my resignation.

"I now write to you my last letter and my farewell.

"In the overwrought and desperate mood in which you found me, it did not seem a sin for me to go away with the man who loved me and whom I loved, before false ideas of life and false ideas of duty made him the husband of another. Conscious that your wife was a hopeless lunatic whose present or future could in no way be influenced by our actions, I reasoned that we wronged no one in taking the happiness so long denied us.

"The last three years of my life have been full of desolation and sorrow. From the day my mother died, the stars of light which had gemmed the firmament for me, seemed one by one to be obliterated, until I stood in utter darkness. You found me in the very blackest hour of all--and you seemed a shining sun to me.

"Yet so soon as my tired brain and sorrow-worn heart were able to think and reason, I realised that it was not the man I had worshipped as an ideal, who had come to me and asked me to lower my standard of womanhood. It was another and less worthy man--and this other was to be my companion through time, and perhaps eternity. When I learned that your insane wife was my sister, and that knowing this fact you yet planned our flight, an indescribable feeling of repulsion awoke in my heart.

"I confess that this arose more from a sentiment than a principle. The relationship of your wife to me made the contemplated sin no greater, but rendered it more tasteless.

"Had I gone away with you as I consented to do, the world would have said, she but follows her fatal inheritance--like mother like daughter. There were some bitter rebellious hours, when that thought came to me. But to-day light has shone upon me, and I know there is a law of Divine Heredity which is greater and more powerful than any tendency we derive from parents or grandparents. I have believed much in creeds all my life; and in the hour of great trials I found I was leaning on broken reeds. I have now ceased to look to men or books for truth--I have found it in my own soul. I acknowledge no unfortunate tendencies from any earthly inheritance; centuries of sinful or weak ancestors are as nothing beside the God within. The divine and immortal ME is older than my ancestral tree; it is as old as the universe. It is as old as the first great Cause of which it is a part. Strong with this consciousness, I am prepared to meet the world alone, and unafraid from this day onward. When I think of the optimistic temperament, the good brain, and the vigorous body which were naturally mine, and then of the wretched being who was my legitimate sister, I know that I was rightly generated, however unfortunately born, just as she was wrongly generated though legally born.

"My father, I am told, married into a family whose crest is traced back to the tenth century. I carry a coat-of-arms older yet--the Cross; it dates back eighteen hundred years--yes, many thousand years, and so I feel myself the nobler of the two. Had you been more of a disciple of Christ, and less of a disciple of man, you would have realised this truth long ago, as I realise it to-day. No man should dare stand before his fellows as a revealer of divine knowledge until he has penetrated the inmost recesses of his own soul, and found God's holy image there; and until he can show others the way to the same wonderful discovery. The God you worshipped was far away in the heavens, so far that he could not come to you and save you from your baser self in the hour of temptation. But the true God has been miraculously revealed to me. He dwells within; one who has found Him, will never debase His temple.

"Though there is no legal obstacle now in the path to our union, there is a spiritual one which is insurmountable. I NO LONGER LOVE YOU. I am sorry for you, but that is all. You belonged to my yesterday--you can have no part in my to-day.

The man who tempted me in my weak hour to go lower, could not help me to go higher. And my face is set toward the heights.

"I must prove to that world that a child born under the shadow of shame, and of two weak, uncontrolled parents, can be virtuous, strong, brave and sensible. That she can conquer passion and impulse, by the use of her divine inheritance of will; and that she can compel the respect of the public by her discreet life and lofty ideals.

"I shall stay in this place until I have vindicated my name and character from every aspersion cast upon them. I shall retain my position of organist, and retain it until I have accumulated sufficient means to go abroad and prepare myself for the musical career in which I know I can excel. I am young, strong and ambitious. My unusual sorrows will give me greater power of character if I accept them as spiritual tonics--bitter but strengthening.

"Farewell, and may God be with you.

"Joy Irving."

When the rector of St Blank's returned from the Beryngford Cemetery, where he had placed the body of his wife beside her father, he found this letter lying on his table in the hotel.

The Codes Of Hammurabi And Moses
W. W. Davies

QTY

The discovery of the Hammurabi Code is one of the greatest achievements of archaeology, and is of paramount interest, not only to the student of the Bible, but also to all those interested in ancient history...

Religion   **ISBN:** *1-59462-338-4*   **Pages:132**

MSRP $12.95

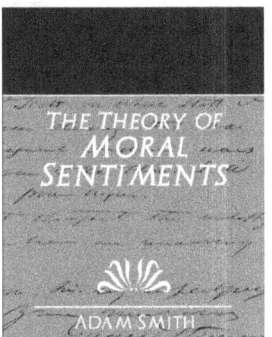

The Theory of Moral Sentiments
Adam Smith

QTY

This work from 1749. contains original theories of conscience amd moral judgment and it is the foundation for systemof morals.

Philosophy   **ISBN:** *1-59462-777-0*   **Pages:536**

MSRP $19.95

Jessica's First Prayer
Hesba Stretton

QTY

In a screened and secluded corner of one of the many railway-bridges which span the streets of London there could be seen a few years ago, from five o'clock every morning until half past eight, a tidily set-out coffee-stall, consisting of a trestle and board, upon which stood two large tin cans, with a small fire of charcoal burning under each so as to keep the coffee boiling during the early hours of the morning when the work-people were thronging into the city on their way to their daily toil...

Pages:84

Childrens   **ISBN:** *1-59462-373-2*   *MSRP $9.95*

My Life and Work
Henry Ford

QTY

Henry Ford revolutionized the world with his implementation of mass production for the Model T automobile. Gain valuable business insight into his life and work with his own auto-biography... "We have only started on our development of our country we have not as yet, with all our talk of wonderful progress, done more than scratch the surface. The progress has been wonderful enough but..."

Pages:300

Biographies/   **ISBN:** *1-59462-198-5*   *MSRP $21.95*

The Art of Cross-Examination
Francis Wellman

QTY

I presume it is the experience of every author, after his first book is published upon an important subject, to be almost overwhelmed with a wealth of ideas and illustrations which could readily have been included in his book, and which to his own mind, at least, seem to make a second edition inevitable. Such certainly was the case with me; and when the first edition had reached its sixth impression in five months, I rejoiced to learn that it seemed to my publishers that the book had met with a sufficiently favorable reception to justify a second and considerably enlarged edition. ..

Reference   ISBN: *1-59462-647-2*

Pages:412

MSRP $19.95

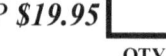

On the Duty of Civil Disobedience
Henry David Thoreau

QTY

Thoreau wrote his famous essay, On the Duty of Civil Disobedience, as a protest against an unjust but popular war and the immoral but popular institution of slave-owning. He did more than write—he declined to pay his taxes, and was hauled off to gaol in consequence. Who can say how much this refusal of his hastened the end of the war and of slavery ?

Law   ISBN: *1-59462-747-9*

Pages:48

MSRP $7.45

Dream Psychology Psychoanalysis for Beginners
Sigmund Freud

QTY

Sigmund Freud, born Sigismund Schlomo Freud (May 6, 1856 - September 23, 1939), was a Jewish-Austrian neurologist and psychiatrist who co-founded the psychoanalytic school of psychology. Freud is best known for his theories of the unconscious mind, especially involving the mechanism of repression; his redefinition of sexual desire as mobile and directed towards a wide variety of objects; and his therapeutic techniques, especially his understanding of transference in the therapeutic relationship and the presumed value of dreams as sources of insight into unconscious desires.

Psychology   ISBN: *1-59462-905-6*

Pages:196

MSRP $15.45

The Miracle of Right Thought
Orison Swett Marden

QTY

Believe with all of your heart that you will do what you were made to do. When the mind has once formed the habit of holding cheerful, happy, prosperous pictures, it will not be easy to form the opposite habit. It does not matter how improbable or how far away this realization may see, or how dark the prospects may be, if we visualize them as best we can, as vividly as possible, hold tenaciously to them and vigorously struggle to attain them, they will gradually become actualized, realized in the life. But a desire, a longing without endeavor, a yearning abandoned or held indifferently will vanish without realization.

Pages:360

Self Help   ISBN: *1-59462-644-8*

MSRP $25.45

QTY

The Rosicrucian Cosmo-Conception Mystic Christianity by **Max Heindel**   ISBN: *1-59462-188-8*   **$38.95**
The Rosicrucian Cosmo-conception is not dogmatic, neither does it appeal to any other authority than the reason of the student. It is: not controversial, but is: sent forth in the, hope that it may help to clear...   New Age/Religion Pages 646

Abandonment To Divine Providence by **Jean-Pierre de Caussade**   ISBN: *1-59462-228-0*   **$25.95**
"The Rev. Jean Pierre de Caussade was one of the most remarkable spiritual writers of the Society of Jesus in France in the 18th Century. His death took place at Toulouse in 1751. His works have gone through many editions and have been republished...   Inspirational/Religion Pages 400

Mental Chemistry by **Charles Haanel**   ISBN: *1-59462-192-6*   **$23.95**
Mental Chemistry allows the change of material conditions by combining and appropriately utilizing the power of the mind. Much like applied chemistry creates something new and unique out of careful combinations of chemicals the mastery of mental chemistry...   New Age Pages 354

The Letters of Robert Browning and Elizabeth Barret Barrett 1845-1846 vol II   ISBN: *1-59462-193-4*   **$35.95**
by **Robert Browning** and **Elizabeth Barrett**   Biographies Pages 596

Gleanings In Genesis (volume I) by **Arthur W. Pink**   ISBN: *1-59462-130-6*   **$27.45**
Appropriately has Genesis been termed "the seed plot of the Bible" for in it we have, in germ form, almost all of the great doctrines which are afterwards fully developed in the books of Scripture which follow...   Religion/Inspirational Pages 420

The Master Key by **L. W. de Laurence**   ISBN: *1-59462-001-6*   **$30.95**
In no branch of human knowledge has there been a more lively increase of the spirit of research during the past few years than in the study of Psychology, Concentration and Mental Discipline. The requests for authentic lessons in Thought Control, Mental Discipline and...   New Age/Business Pages 422

The Lesser Key Of Solomon Goetia by **L. W. de Laurence**   ISBN: *1-59462-092-X*   **$9.95**
This translation of the first book of the "Lernegton" which is now for the first time made accessible to students of Talismanic Magic was done, after careful collation and edition, from numerous Ancient Manuscripts in Hebrew, Latin, and French...   New Age/Occult Pages 92

Rubaiyat Of Omar Khayyam by **Edward Fitzgerald**   ISBN:*1-59462-332-5*   **$13.95**
Edward Fitzgerald, whom the world has already learned, in spite of his own efforts to remain within the shadow of anonymity, to look upon as one of the rarest poets of the century, was born at Bredfield, in Suffolk, on the 31st of March, 1809. He was the third son of John Purcell...   Music Pages 172

Ancient Law by **Henry Maine**   ISBN: *1-59462-128-4*   **$29.95**
The chief object of the following pages is to indicate some of the earliest ideas of mankind, as they are reflected in Ancient Law, and to point out the relation of those ideas to modern thought.   Religiom/History Pages 452

Far-Away Stories by **William J. Locke**   ISBN: *1-59462-129-2*   **$19.45**
"Good wine needs no bush, but a collection of mixed vintages does. And this book is just such a collection. Some of the stories I do not want to remain buried for ever in the museum files of dead magazine-numbers an author's not unpardonable vanity..."   Fiction Pages 272

Life of David Crockett by **David Crockett**   ISBN: *1-59462-250-7*   **$27.45**
"Colonel David Crockett was one of the most remarkable men of the times in which he lived. Born in humble life, but gifted with a strong will, an indomitable courage, and unremitting perseverance...   Biographies/New Age Pages 424

Lip-Reading by **Edward Nitchie**   ISBN: *1-59462-206-X*   **$25.95**
Edward B. Nitchie, founder of the New York School for the Hard of Hearing, now the Nitchie School of Lip-Reading, Inc, wrote "LIP-READING Principles and Practice". The development and perfecting of this meritorious work on lip-reading was an undertaking...   How-to Pages 400

A Handbook of Suggestive Therapeutics, Applied Hypnotism, Psychic Science   ISBN: *1-59462-214-0*   **$24.95**
by **Henry Munro**   Health/New Age/Health/Self-help Pages 376

A Doll's House: and Two Other Plays by **Henrik Ibsen**   ISBN: *1-59462-112-8*   **$19.95**
Henrik Ibsen created this classic when in revolutionary 1848 Rome. Introducing some striking concepts in playwriting for the realist genre, this play has been studied the world over.   Fiction/Classics/Plays 308

The Light of Asia by **sir Edwin Arnold**   ISBN: *1-59462-204-3*   **$13.95**
In this poetic masterpiece, Edwin Arnold describes the life and teachings of Buddha. The man who was to become known as Buddha to the world was born as Prince Gautama of India but he rejected the worldly riches and abandoned the reigns of power when...   Religion/History/Biographies Pages 170

The Complete Works of Guy de Maupassant by **Guy de Maupassant**   ISBN: *1-59462-157-8*   **$16.95**
"For days and days, nights and nights, I had dreamed of that first kiss which was to consecrate our engagement, and I knew not on what spot I should put my lips..."   Fiction/Classics Pages 240

The Art of Cross-Examination by **Francis L. Wellman**   ISBN: *1-59462-309-0*   **$26.95**
Written by a renowned trial lawyer, Wellman imparts his experience and uses case studies to explain how to use psychology to extract desired information through questioning.   How-to/Science/Reference Pages 408

Answered or Unanswered? by **Louisa Vaughan**   ISBN: *1-59462-248-5*   **$10.95**
Miracles of Faith in China   Religion Pages 112

The Edinburgh Lectures on Mental Science (1909) by **Thomas**   ISBN: *1-59462-008-3*   **$11.95**
This book contains the substance of a course of lectures recently given by the writer in the Queen Street Hall, Edinburgh. Its purpose is to indicate the Natural Principles governing the relation between Mental Action and Material Conditions...   New Age/Psychology Pages 148

Ayesha by **H. Rider Haggard**   ISBN: *1-59462-301-5*   **$24.95**
Verily and indeed it is the unexpected that happens! Probably if there was one person upon the earth from whom the Editor of this, and of a certain previous history, did not expect to hear again...   Classics Pages 380

Ayala's Angel by **Anthony Trollope**   ISBN: *1-59462-352-X*   **$29.95**
The two girls were both pretty, but Lucy who was twenty-one who supposed to be simple and comparatively unattractive, whereas Ayala was credited, as her Bombwhat romantic name might show, with poetic charm and a taste for romance. Ayala when her father died was nineteen...   Fiction Pages 484

The American Commonwealth by **James Bryce**   ISBN: *1-59462-286-8*   **$34.45**
An interpretation of American democratic political theory. It examines political mechanics and society from the perspective of Scotsman James Bryce   Politics Pages 572

Stories of the Pilgrims by **Margaret P. Pumphrey**   ISBN: *1-59462-116-0*   **$17.95**
This book explores pilgrims religious oppression in England as well as their escape to Holland and eventual crossing to America on the Mayflower, and their early days in New England...   History Pages 268

QTY

The Fasting Cure by *Sinclair Upton*   ISBN: *1-59462-222-1* **$13.95**

In the Cosmopolitan Magazine for May, 1910, and in the Contemporary Review (London) for April, 1910, I published an article dealing with my experiences in fasting. I have written a great many magazine articles, but never one which attracted so much attention... New Age/Self Help/Health Pages 164

Hebrew Astrology by *Sepharial*   ISBN: *1-59462-308-2* **$13.45**

In these days of advanced thinking it is a matter of common observation that we have left many of the old landmarks behind and that we are now pressing forward to greater heights and to a wider horizon than that which represented the mind-content of our progenitors... Astrology Pages 144

Thought Vibration or The Law of Attraction in the Thought World   ISBN: *1-59462-127-6* **$12.95**

by *William Walker Atkinson*   Psychology/Religion Pages 144

Optimism by *Helen Keller*   ISBN: *1-59462-108-X* **$15.95**

Helen Keller was blind, deaf, and mute since 19 months old, yet famously learned how to overcome these handicaps, communicate with the world, and spread her lectures promoting optimism. An inspiring read for everyone... Biographies/Inspirational Pages 84

Sara Crewe by *Frances Burnett*   ISBN: *1-59462-360-0* **$9.45**

In the first place, Miss Minchin lived in London. Her home was a large, dull, tall one, in a large, dull square, where all the houses were alike, and all the sparrows were alike, and where all the door-knockers made the same heavy sound... Childrens/Classic Pages 88

The Autobiography of Benjamin Franklin by *Benjamin Franklin*   ISBN: *1-59462-135-7* **$24.95**

The Autobiography of Benjamin Franklin has probably been more extensively read than any other American historical work, and no other book of its kind has had such ups and downs of fortune. Franklin lived for many years in England, where he was agent... Biographies/History Pages 332

Name	
Email	
Telephone	
Address	
City, State ZIP	

☐ **Credit Card**   ☐ **Check / Money Order**

Credit Card Number	
Expiration Date	
Signature	

Please Mail to: Book Jungle
PO Box 2226
Champaign, IL 61825
or Fax to: 630-214-0564

ORDERING INFORMATION

web: *www.bookjungle.com*
email: *sales@bookjungle.com*
fax: *630-214-0564*
mail: *Book Jungle PO Box 2226 Champaign, IL 61825*
or PayPal *to sales@bookjungle.com*

Please contact us for bulk discounts

DIRECT-ORDER TERMS

**20% Discount if You Order
Two or More Books**
Free Domestic Shipping!
Accepted: Master Card, Visa,
Discover, American Express